KILLER LAKE

DAVID BENTON
AND
W.D. GAGLIANI

deadite
press

deadite press

DEADITE PRESS
P.O. BOX 10065
PORTLAND, OR 97296
www.DEADITEPRESS.com

AN ERASERHEAD PRESS COMPANY
www.ERASERHEADPRESS.com

ISBN: 978-1-62105-306-4

Kiler Lake copyright © 2019 by David Benton and
W.D. Gagliani

Cover design by Deadite Press

Printed in the USA.

Acknowledgments

Benton & Gagliani would like to thank some of our influences: Dario Argento, Clive Barker, David Benton, John Carpenter, Don Coscarelli, Wes Craven, W.D. Gagliani, Stuart Gordon, James Herbert, Tobe Hooper, Jack Ketchum, Stephen King, Joe Lansdale, Richard Laymon, Edward Lee, Robert R. McCammon, George Romero, David J. Schow, John Skipp, Craig Spector.

PREGAME

The celebrants filed into the damp chamber. Hoods up, hiding most of their features in shadow, and bodies naked under the sheer black robes, their hands held sputtering black candles.

They were thirty-nine in number—thirteen times three, a triumvirate coven—and they flowed around the still figure of their leader, who stood just within the chamber's open heavy brass doors.

Their leader called himself the Beast after his claimed ancestor, Aleister Crowley. He had lived much of his life in honor of his forebear, following the Way. He wore a robe as well, but his was blood-red and instead of a peaked hood his head was covered by a monstrous cowl that was formed from a hollowed goat's head, its horns extending eighteen inches forward of the former animal's bony forehead. His eyes were just barely visible behind the bleached eye-sockets of the grotesque mask that had been passed down through the generations. His lower jaw was visible beneath the goat's snout, and his jet-black goatee gave him the satanic countenance he cultivated.

They circled the chipped altar carved out of stone that rose from the floor of the chamber. Next to the altar was a lower stone platform on which a thin layer of black leather had been stretched and tied like a corset. The celebrants left one side of the circle open so their leader could turn and face them as well as tonight's focus of their rite. When they had all filed inside, he closed the massive doors with a deep booming sound and turned the elaborate brass key in the lock, then made the key disappear under his robes.

First the Beast led them on a series of chants they had learned years ago, painfully dissonant chants that were almost a parody of the beautiful Gregorian chants usually sung by monks.

Candles flickered in the slight breeze that flowed from hidden passages and tunnels. In sconces set at the four compass points, large torches burned aromatically and provided most of the chamber's light. The pillars that lined the two longer sides of the stone and marble room cast deep shadows from which the occasional shuffle or shamble seemed to come. The celebrants were accustomed to the feeling of being watched, although they had never seen anyone other than their fellow members. They were used to the rising and falling whispers that swirled about their ears. But now even the whispers seemed to fade out.

After the last chant echoed to silence, the Beast faced his coven and raised his hands.

"I welcome you to the most important ritual of our long history. You have all worked hard to lead us to this day, and our efforts here will benefit us all in ways we can barely begin to imagine. Tonight we pool the strength of our spirits, as we have prepared to do for many years. Tonight is the night of our destiny. Behold, the Summoning!"

The torches and candles flared to three times their size. Wind gusted loudly through the chamber. A shiver seemed to flow through every body, as the presence of something of great power made itself known to them.

"Prepare the altar!" shouted the Beast, his arms spread overhead. His voice bounced off the slick walls.

A woman nearby dropped her hood, revealing long, raven-black hair, sharp but sensual features, red lips and dark-rimmed eyes. As the others looked on from beneath their hoods, she undid the rope belt and let the robe slide off her naked body. Her breasts were full, nipples hard in the cool breeze, thrusting upward proudly at the lust she felt while trapped in the many male and female gazes.

Two others took her arms and helped her straddle the

leather stone, stretching her face down across its width so her hands hung down to the floor. Her spread-eagled form was like a starfish at the center of the circle.

The Beast approached from behind, his robe dropping to the chamber floor. His lust was evident from the erection that bobbed in front of his powerful loins.

The time for ritual had arrived.

He took the woman from behind with a grunt, while several other celebrants shed their robes and prepared to join in. Soon the "altar" was the center of a swirling and ever-changing group of grunting, thrusting, sighing, and screaming members of the coven, both male and female, and the woman struggled to keep up with her genitals, her hands, her mouth, and even her feet.

The *sex magick* ritual continued until the Beast, who had stepped away momentarily, returned for his climax. He grunted and his precious seed flowed over the flesh of the altar.

The naked bodies of his followers were entwined all around the living altar now, at his feet, over and above and below the trembling flesh of the woman whose body was the conduit to the Underworld that the Beast's chanting had opened.

The Beast's voice rose above the lustful din of his flock. The timing was important.

"Bring the child!"

A long, tapered dagger had suddenly appeared in his hands. It glinted in the fire and candlelight. The woman who was the altar raised her head, her eyelids hooded and mascara streaked. "Master," she said, her voice wheedling and hoarse from the many uses of her open jaw, "my brother took the baby today..." Her words stilled the sounds of her fellow coven members, whose sudden silence became ominous.

"You promised our Lord Asmodeus your first-born,

Sister!" the Beast's voice enunciated clearly, slowly, not unkindly. *A misunderstanding, perhaps,* he seemed to be saying. Reminding her as a friend of her promise.

"I did, Master," said the woman after hesitating. "But my brother must have...learned of our meeting. I—I don't know how. But I have brought you...a substitute."

She raised her body from its supine position and gestured toward the rear of the chamber, where a pet carrier had been resting unnoticed until now.

The Beast glared at the woman. "Bring it to me," he thundered. Any implied kindness had left his tone. The dagger's tip danced dangerously close to human flesh as if it were drawn there, powered by his anger.

Two naked celebrants carried the crate and laid it at his feet. One withdrew from it a fussing baby, presumably someone else's. The baby started to squeal.

"This is not your child!" the Beast snarled at the woman, whose eyes had widened. She struggled to rise, but her sweaty, semen-streaked body was held down by two men and two women, celebrants turned captors. "The compact was sealed!" he thundered. "The ritual is clear and cannot be altered. Without the promised blood, we will not be gifted with the benevolent arrival of our Lord Asmodeus. This means you have failed me! You have failed your coven. You have failed your Lord of demons!"

"No!" the woman whimpered. "No, this child is —"

"Not of your blood!" the Beast shouted. "I can smell *it*, and it is not of the promised strain. Take it away and kill it like a dog!"

"But wait, Master," she pleaded. A look of horror crossed her face. Sudden fear. "Asmodeus need not know!"

"Fool!" their leader shouted above the gusting winds swirling throughout the chamber. "You cannot deceive the Deceiver! Now my servants, remove this life from our circle!"

Someone hastened to follow his orders, another blade flashing silver until it turned red and silenced the tiny squalling voice.

The woman who had brought the baby shuddered, but not because of its fate—she shuddered because she suddenly saw her own fate all too clearly. She tried to rise up and step away from the smothering circle, but the hands holding her down were too strong.

"And now," the Beast leaned into her, hissing, "there is only one way to salvage the ritual! With blood from the promised child's bloodline. It's all right, Sister, the sacrifice must have personal meaning. We must lose in order to gain. That is the meaning of sacrifice."

"Nooooooo!" The woman's voice rose but was smothered by the chanting of the celebrants, who stood as close as they could get to the altar, where her flesh quivered repeatedly now as her muscles contracted, and she struggled, her limbs spread out painfully in four directions. "Please, Seb..."

The Beast cut her off with a glare that sliced through her even though she couldn't see his eyes beneath the mask. Speaking their birth names within the sacrificial chamber was forbidden. He raised the dagger over his head.

Desperately she cried, "But it wasn't my fault, Master! My brother..."

Her pleas were cut short as the dagger fell once, twice, three times, and the chant accompanied his violent motions as the blood flowed and splattered, anointing those fortunate enough to be nearby.

The woman's screams rose to a crescendo, but faded to a painful keening as the blade sank into her flesh again and again. Blood flowed freely from the many wounds, staining the blade crimson.

When the Beast gestured, the ragged doll-like body was released and tipped. Cups and chalices appeared and caught dribbles of the woman's hot blood, then were passed around from celebrant to celebrant. They paused only to sip from the steaming cups, then continued the sacrificial chant.

The Beast stepped back and watched over his flock as the sacrifice was fulfilled despite the betrayer's last-second attempt to shirk her duty. He thought about the child. Where had she stashed it? Perhaps it would be best to find it and let it suffer the same fate as its cursed mother as soon as possible. But now the Beast smiled grimly as his followers became drunk on the woman's essence after having used her as receptacle for theirs. By now robes had been shucked and sexual acts were breaking out everywhere in the chamber, by twos and threes and fours. Arms, legs, breasts, and genitalia intertwined and blurred as the rhythm of the feast increased in tempo.

The gusts of wind that had begun to blow through the chamber also increased their intensity, the pillars creating an inhuman wailing sound that served as soundtrack to the obscene festivities. The flames burned brightly, then were suddenly snuffed out. The celebrants paused in their blood-drunk revelry to note that they could no longer see.

And then a glow arose from behind them and reached for the rocky ceiling, spreading out over them like a cloud formation in the throes of the northern lights.

The Beast raised his spread arms and opened his hands.

"Lord Asmodeus!" he cried out, a smile creeping across his features under the mask. "You have come!"

FIRST
QUARTER

CHAPTER ONE

Twenty-Five Years Later

She leaned in through the open driver's side door and placed the sweating water bottle in the cup holder. In her mind, she was running inventory and hoping they weren't forgetting anything.

Straightening, Mandi intentionally caught a glimpse of herself in the vanity mirror on the underside of the sun visor.

Vain! She smiled at herself and tucked a wayward strand of her dishwater-blond hair over her ear. She heard a loud *thump* behind her, pulled herself reluctantly away from the mirror, and searched for the source of the commotion.

Her friend Anna stood over her oversized and overstuffed suitcase in the driveway, jettisoned dramatically seconds before, and let out an exaggerated sigh. "I hope we have room for this," she declared. Her hand rested on her hip while the breeze tousled her obsidian black curls, making them dance in front of her mirror-lensed aviators. The glasses complemented her perfectly bronzed face— product of her proud Puerto Rican heritage—and gave her a mysterious, exotic air.

"Jesus, Anna! We're only going away for the weekend!"

"Yeah well, you never know what you might need."

"What do you *have* in there?"

"Just essentials: clothes, shoes, makeup, curling iron, clothes iron, blow dryer..."

"You know we're going camping, right?" Then: "*Clothes iron?*"

Anna shrugged, implying that it shouldn't make any difference. Needs are needs.

"Fine," Mandi said, her shoulders slumping in surrender. "Let's see if it fits."

She grasped the bag's handle and dragged it on its tiny wheels to the back of the silver Nissan SUV. The hatch was already open, the back crammed full of rolled sleeping bags, plus a tent, a couple of duffel bags, and a large red cooler stuffed with food and drinks.

Mandi stared at the load, then sighed quietly. "I guess if we move a few things..."

"We could just leave my sleeping bag here." Krystal had suddenly appeared at Mandi's side. Her platinum hair was freshly cropped short, pixie style, and her half-shirt exposed her impressive abdominal muscles, not to mention the lower part of her breasts.

"What, are you and your rock-hard abs and boobs just going to sleep on the ground?"

"No," Krystal said patiently, ignoring the jab. "Jason said that there was a big cabin there. Almost like a resort. With a hot tub and a speedboat and...*everything.* I'll just sleep in a bed."

"Yeah, but there are going to be a lot of people there. This is gonna be a huge party. There might not be room for you. They said bring stuff for camping. Maybe the beds are already spoken for."

"Oh, I'll find a bed," Krystal said, her eyes gleaming impishly.

"Krystal!" Anna screeched. "You're such a slut!"

"Look who's talking! Besides, I'm not a slut...I'm a *sex machine.*"

They all laughed at the familiar line.

"Well, just in case we'll keep the sleeping bags and

make room for Anna's things," said Mandi finally. "Maybe Jason's grandparents are staying in the bedrooms," she added, beginning to shuffle the contents of the SUV with the methodical creativity. "I am the master packer."

"Yeah, but you're not as rich as Seinfeld."

"True."

"So," Krystal said a moment later, "are we seriously picking up Dummy Wallace?"

"His name is *Danny*, Krystal. And yes, we're picking him up. They said the party's for the football team and he's on the team."

"He's not *on* the team," Anna said. "He's the assistant equipment manager. He doesn't even actually go to class."

"Right?" Krystal added, nodding. "Jason's gonna be pissed."

Mandi sighed. "Why would he be pissed? It's a party. There'll be a ton of people there who aren't even invited. Jason probably won't even notice."

"He'll be pissed because that's the point, he *didn't* invite Danny, that's why."

"Besides, he's slow. And he creeps me out," Anna said.

"He's not slow. Okay, maybe he is a *little* slow. But he's medicated. And he had a hard upbringing...without his parents and stuff."

"How do you know all this?" Krystal asked.

"He's Professor Wallace's nephew."

Anna and Krystal stared at Mandi, blinking.

"You know, Professor Wallace—I was in his parapsychology class last semester. He told me that Danny's parents died when he was really little, and he came to live with the professor. I guess whatever happened really traumatized him. He couldn't even talk for the longest time. Now the university pays him to help with some kind of research and Professor Wallace got the coach to let him help out with the team."

Krystal and Anna looked each other up and down before Krystal said, "I think she's got the hots for him."

Anna nodded her agreement.

"Oh, come on you guys. Danny doesn't have any friends outside of the guys on the team."

"He doesn't have any friends outside of *you*, Mandi," said Anna.

"Help me with this ridiculous bag," Mandi said abruptly, turning to Anna, and the two girls hefted its weight with a united *Grunt!* into the space Mandi had carved out for it, patting it into place until it fit snugly. "I guess that's it then," she said.

"That's it," Krystal agreed.

"So are we ready to go?" Mandi asked.

"I guess so," said Anna. "So we're gonna go pick up Dummy...er, I mean *Danny*?"

"Yup."

"Then I wanna ride shotgun. I told you, that guy freaks me out."

"Fine," Krystal said with a frown. "But if he gets weird I'm gonna bust him in his shit."

"He won't get weird. He probably won't even say a word. All right, let's go."

"Road trip!" chanted Krystal and Anna in unison as they piled into the SUV.

CHAPTER TWO

Professor Tim Wallace tried measuring his words as he stood at the kitchen counter sipping a tall glass of ice water. He longed for a drink of something stronger, but he held out.

In the room's silence, the ticking of his many collected old-fashioned clocks seemed as loud as church bells pealing. He wasn't sure what to tell Danny, and the ticking was an ever-present reminder that time was slipping away. Of course, he'd known this day was coming. Danny wasn't a child anymore. But he still needed help and supervision at least part of the time, in case of emergencies. The dread was making the professor's stomach knot up, and that was making him crave a drink. *Not for the first time.*

"I'm ready to go, Uncle Tim," Danny called out from the dining room.

Here goes... The professor set his glass down on the counter and went over to Danny who was seated at the dining room table, drumming nervously with his fingers on the table top. "Do you really have to do this?" he asked.

Danny looked up. "W-w-what do you mean?"

"I mean, do you have to go on this trip, Danny? I would rather you didn't. I think you should stay home this weekend and we'll go to a movie or something. You know, something fun for a change."

"N-n-n-no, Uncle Tim, I want to go camping. To the team party."

"Yes, I know..." The professor pulled out a chair and sat down, swimming in the cheap suit jacket he wore over an aged *Iron Maiden* t-shirt. "But I'm not sure if you're ready for this yet, Danny. A party with adults...well, basically adults. Barely adults. Things happen, Danny. Bad things happen when people drink and lose control." *I should know.* "I just wish you would reconsider."

"But, M-M-Mandi invited me." Danny's dark eyes surveyed the floor.

Professor Wallace sighed.

Women!

And of course Danny's stammer was getting worse, as it always did when he was under stress.

The professor took a deep, calming breath before continuing. "Yes, I know Danny, but she doesn't know about your...condition. I'm afraid something might happen to you, something bad. I'd rather you stayed here where we can make sure...nothing happens to you." He reached out a finger to tip up his nephew's chin. But he never got there.

"*No*, Uncle Tim! I'm going!"

Danny's loud refusal was punctuated by the sound of shattering glass coming from the kitchen.

Wallace snapped his neck in that direction. He could see through the open doorway that the glass he'd left on the counter was now on the floor in a thousand pieces. He inhaled slowly through his nose.

"I'm an a-a-a-adult now, Uncle Tim." Danny continued, more collected now. He'd ignored the breaking glass. "You can't keep m-m-me here. I want to go to the party."

Tim Wallace sighed. Of course he couldn't keep his nephew in the house forever. *Which was more dangerous?* "Did you take your medication?"

"Yes."

Outside, a car horn tooted. Professor Wallace glanced out the window at the silver SUV that had pulled up to the curb. *Great timing. I lost this argument before it began.*

"Well, here's your ride, Danny."

"Okay, Uncle Tim!" Danny paused, smiling shyly. "Thank you."

Both men rose from their chairs.

"Do you have your phone?"

Danny tapped his pocket. "Yes."

"You'll be back Sunday night?"

"Yes, Uncle Tim."

"Call me if you need anything. Or if you just want to talk."

"I will, I promise!"

"I love you, Danny."

"Love you too, Uncle Tim." Danny picked up his backpack and sleeping bag.

The professor walked his nephew to the door, watched him walk out to the waiting car, and—even though he wasn't in any normal way a religious man—he prayed.

CHAPTER THREE

A half hour into the drive, the conversation—which had been admittedly shallow—dried up and the three women and Danny sat in relative silence.

From behind the wheel, Mandi's thoughts drifted to the subject of Tyler. She couldn't wait to see him, to revel in the security she felt when she was wrapped up in his muscular arms, to feel his touch. To smell him. She liked to fantasize about their possible future together and though he hadn't proposed or anything, she liked to try his surname on for size—to see how it fit—in her imagination. She knew she wasn't going to keep her own name because Swartzenburger was way too...ugly. In fact, she'd always hated it. Sounded like greasy food. Greasy German food, no less.

To her right, Anna seemed comfortably contorted while painting her nails a deep shade of red, head bobbing to whatever was playing in her earbuds.

In the backseat, Krystal sat texting someone—or *everyone*—sharing pictures of sights in and out of the car during their drive, and updating all her many social networks. Danny sat quietly next to her, mostly looking down at his feet.

Mandi felt a little guilty about having invited him. She worried that he wouldn't fit in after all. And the other girls' reaction to him didn't help her feel any better. Why did they behave that way? She just didn't get it. After all, Danny was harmless. And he was a nice enough guy. And she almost hated to admit it, but if it wasn't for his speech impediment and his social awkwardness, he would be kind of hot. He was tall and lean but muscular, with a mop of unkempt black hair and the sweetest brown eyes—like a doe, or lamb. Despite his boyish demeanor, on the outside he was all man; she wondered about his "equipment" and chuckled to herself.

They sped along the winding rural highway, two lanes of slick blacktop with freshly painted lane markings, surrounded by farm fields that alternated with unmanaged woodlands. Rarely did Mandi see another vehicle, and when she did it was almost a guarantee that it would be either a dusty pickup truck or a deathly-slow tractor to speed around. Almost before she knew it—with Tyler's rock-hard body very prominently on her mind—the sun had transitioned from its late morning position high in the sky to the side slant of early afternoon, and the miles had slipped past the racing Nissan. Inside, the conversation had stuttered, faltered and died a half-dozen times, before finally crashing to an awkward halt.

Now Mandi picked up her water bottle and tried to coax another sip of lukewarm water from it, unsuccessfully.

Just then, she spotted an old rusted sign at the side of the road: *Bobby's Gas Station and Bait Shop 5 Miles Ahead.*

"You guys need to stop for anything?" she asked. " 'Cause we could use some gas and I need something to drink. Right after I pee."

"About time," Krystal said. "Do you suppose they have a somewhat clean bathroom?"

"I sure hope so," Mandi added. "But if not there's always the woods."

"Well, if that's the case, I'll hold it. I don't need a spider crawling up my butt while I'm trying to pee. Or worse."

Mandi looked over at Anna who was now dozing, earbuds still stuffed into her ears. She reached over and plucked one out. Anna flinched. "What?" she whined sleepily.

"We're stopping to get gas and use the bathroom."

Anna nodded. "Kay."

"You okay with that, Danny?" Mandi looked back at him in the mirror.

Danny nodded silently, his eyes catching Mandi's in the reflection. He smiled weakly and she gave him a smile back. *Poor kid, stuck in here with these two.* She did *not* include herself.

Emerging from a forested bend where the trees draped their shadows over the highway, Mandi finally spotted the gas station heralded by the battered sign. Five miles had seemed to stretch forever as the trees thickened on both sides of the road. There was a brief stretch of service road to navigate first. The sign perfectly matched the dilapidated building with two ancient-looking, rusty pumps lined up out in front of grime-streaked windows, squatting at the crossroads of the main stretch of highway and the dirt service road that cut across it almost diagonally. On the other side of the road a weathered farmhouse seemed to have sagged between a pair of enormous weeping willows, the long branches of which whipped across the house's irregularly patched roof. As she glanced at the farmhouse, thinking it had to be long unoccupied, she thought she spotted a figure, or a shadow, at the side of one of the crooked second-floor windows. It was hard to say because the figure, if that's what it was, disappeared almost immediately. Mandi shook her head. *Spooky place.* She pulled into the gas station's bumpy lot, feeling a tingle in the back of her neck as if that person in the house was staring at *her* even though she was nearly invisible in the driver's seat. Despite the warm weather, she shivered. The decades-old concrete—which was crumbling in some spots—crunched under the Nissan's weight as she sidled it up to one of the rickety pumps.

Jesus, she thought, *can this place look any weirder?*

26

They all got out of the Nissan and stretched. Then Mandi popped the gas cap, lifted the nozzle from the decrepit pump, and started filling the tank. Amazingly, it worked and the old-fashioned metal number plates in the cracked window display started rolling up her purchase price.

"Look at this dump," Krystal said as if reading Mandi's mind, admiring the cinderblock station while arching the stiffness from her back. "I feel like we just time traveled into the Fifties."

"Eighteen Fifties?" quipped Anna.

"Very funny. This is at least post-war. *Civil War*."

"Yeah, I know," said Mandi. "They only have one kind of gas...regular. Weird. Hey, I hope they take credit cards. Or even know what they are."

"Everybody takes credit cards, sweetie," Anna said. As an avid user herself, she knew that very well.

Mandi shrugged and let the gas flow noisily.

She couldn't help but notice that neither of her friends were talking to Danny, who just stood and stared at the blocky gas station. She also noticed that no one was in a rush to go into the building. "Krystal, I thought you had to go to the bathroom?" Krystal was milling around and kicking weeds that grew up through jagged cracks in the concrete.

"I might be better off using the woods," Krystal said, and she sounded serious.

Amazingly the pump automatically shut off and Mandi replaced the nozzle. Then she read the total, shrugged and headed inside. The others hesitated behind her, so she turned around and walked backward. "Come on, guys," she said, hoping for some support. She eyed the abandoned-looking building critically—with its faded hand-painted signs in the window, one of which seemed to read *Nightcrawlers* with a double-L and another *Open*. "I'm *not* going in there alone."

"I-I-I'll go with you, Mandi," said Danny.

"A gentleman," Mandi replied, smiling. "Thank you, Danny."

"Me too," Anna said quickly.

"Yeah, okay," Krystal added, rolling her eyes.

Mandi suspected they didn't like their only male guardian abandoning them. She didn't blame them and let the joke die on her lips.

As she entered through the screen door—which, she noted, was propped open with an old-fashioned milk can—Mandi noticed a paper wasps' nest just inside the wind-crinkled awning above the door. She ducked instinctively, though the two wasps in evidence didn't seem aggressive.

Inside, the place was cramped and poorly lit, with natural light barely streaming in from outside through the grime providing the only illumination. A long wooden counter took up most of one side, with an antique cash register near the front and a door behind it. Plastic jars of candy took up the remainder of the counter space: gummy bears, root beer barrels, lemon drops, and other types of innumerable variety, as well as beef sticks and other snacks. Near the walls were dingy display racks of potato chips, pretzels, and candy popcorn, all seeming stuck in an earlier decade. Beside those were shelves full of greasy motor oil cans, fishing lures, and most unusually, condoms. And there was one glass-fronted cooler of indeterminate age filled with bottled soda of a regional brand name Mandi had never seen, apparently Paramount. It hummed like an industrial air conditioner from the Fifties.

"Where's the damn bathroom?" Krystal said, squinting in the gloom.

Mandi shrugged. Then she called out, "Is anyone here?"

No one answered.

They rambled around the old, dusty store. Danny eyed the potato chip display with equal parts hunger and trepidation. Krystal sighed with her hands on her hips. Anna picked up a package of ribbed Trojans: "Do these things expire?" she asked.

"I brought some," Krystal said. "From this century."

Mandi's attention was drawn to the pile of thin local newspapers scattered on the counter. The cover of the top issue bore a picture of cows standing in a barnyard. The headline read: *Sheriff Disputes Claims of Cattle Mutilation.*

She scanned the article, smirking.

While local farmer Eli Little swears that the dead steer found in his field last week looked like the work of a "mad butcher," local authorities say otherwise.

Sheriff John Kramer of Lakeland County maintains it looks like the work of a large predator. "We've had reports of bears in this area over the past few months and that's what we think we have here," he told state and county reporters. "These bears are generally not a danger to people, but they should not be approached. Obviously they are hungry and potentially dangerous. If you see one please call the sheriff's department. Do not try and confront it on your own."

This is contrary to various reports last week of potential cult activity in the area, which the sheriff was quick to discount.

"We've heard a lot of people talking about strange happenings, from Satan worshipers to alien invasions and that's just a load of manure," Sheriff Kramer said when approached for comment.

But a search of local records shows...

"It's out back," a gravelly voice said from nearby.

Mandi jumped. She looked up and suddenly as if seemingly out of nowhere there was now a bent old man behind the counter, his face bristling with gray whiskers. His crooked teeth looked like yellow beans.

Mandi was struck dumb by the silence of his arrival.

Obviously he had come through the doorway behind the counter, but she hadn't heard or seen him. And yet there he was.

"Somebody asked about a bathroom?" the man said irritably.

All these interruptions must be tough. Great-grampa needs his toilet time.

"Yeah, I did," Krystal said, raising her hand like a kindergartener on a class tour.

"Well, it's out back. Nothin' special mind you, just a one-seater. Got some newspaper and such in there." He pointed to where Mandi had been looking. "Also several examples of our fine daily right next to the pot. And no, *those* don't have an expiration date...or least, I don't believe they do. Then again, it's been awhile since I had any need to worry about that. Not many visitors such as your fine selves."

Mandi slapped a credit card in front of the old man. "Gas," she said with difficulty, as if her mouth was filled with rocks. "I got gas."

"Sounds like a personal problem," the old man chuckled obscenely, sneering.

As he scooped the card off the counter, Mandi noticed that he was missing the first two fingers of his right hand. Somehow this fact made the old man seem even more sinister than his abrupt arrival.

"So, where you folks headed?" He looked at the card suspiciously, as if was an artifact. From the future.

"Killdeer Lake," Mandi managed. What was with the third degree? And why the hell weren't her friends piping up? She started to look around, but his gaze held her in place.

"Oh, with all the little rich kids, hun?" he said, and she wasn't sure if he'd called her *hun* or if he'd said *huh*.

Mandi didn't know what to say. She was put off by the question's implications. She and her friends weren't *rich kids*. Sure, they were better off than some (maybe most) but they certainly weren't rich. More like upper middle class. What was left of it.

"Yeah," she said with a chuckle. *Better to humor the old bastard. No real point debating his deeply held views.*

"Just be careful up there," the man said, sounding as if he were about to spit. He was flipping through a thick floppy book of numbers, comparing her credit card number to the tiny columns. Geez, did they even still make those, since the...*Seventies*?

"Because of the bears?" she asked, remembering the newspaper article. She hated being alone with this guy. Just where the hell *were* her friends?

"Bears!" the man ridiculed. "Where'd you get such a dumb idea? I mean be careful of the lake. Every couple of years some dumb rich kid disappears up there by that lake. Never heard of again. Vanished. That lake's so dang deep and cold it keeps its secrets and keeps 'em deep." Now he handed back her card after doing something to it under the counter, out of her view.

"Thanks," Mandi said reluctantly, trying not to let him touch her fingers. Then she backed away and when she turned there were Anna and Danny, their eyes wide and beckoning. *Really? Danny I could understand, but Anna?* They turned away and walked through the propped door. Krystal was already outside, waiting.

"How'd you get out here?" Mandi said.

"That was weird," Anna added, speaking over Mandi. "That old perv was listening to us from the back room. I bet he's back there now, spanking his... whatever. Thinking of our sweet young flesh."

"Yeah, right? What a creeper," Krystal said. "Looked at us like he's never seen chicks. And a guy with chicks," she added, winking at Danny, who blushed.

"How was the bathroom?" Mandi asked.

"Disgusting. You don't wanna know. I lost the need. Literally just vanished. Waiting until we get to Jason's. I'd rather risk a blown bladder than one of a thousand possible diseases and bacterial infections. Not to mention splinters… and spider bites. Big honkin' spiders, I'm sayin'."

"Ew," said Mandi and Anna in unison. Even Danny's face went ashen. *Who likes spiders?*

"Is that where the smell is coming from?" Anna asked.

"I know, right?" said Krystal.

"It smells like bigfoot's dick," Mandi said with a smile, quoting one of their favorite movies. They all laughed. Danny somewhat uncertainly.

Suddenly no one's bladder was complaining.

They piled back into the Nissan. In a minute they were following the winding narrow service road, then pulling back out onto the highway. Mandi checked the GPS, which was momentarily confused. "Only thirteen more miles to Killdeer Lake," she announced when the satellite figured out where they'd gone.

Somehow, as they'd pulled out she had managed to avoid looking at the weird-ass farmhouse across the way. She didn't want to see the curtain raised and a figure peering out at them. But she thought she'd felt the staring, anyway.

She shivered.

CHAPTER FOUR

The signs for the Killdeer Lake public beach and boat access had been vandalized, Mandi noted as she motored past them. Someone had scratched out the *d* and the first *e*, so it now read: *Killer Lake*.

Damn vandals. There had always been problems in the area with kids painting over and altering signs, and even shooting at traffic signs until every stop sign in the county was perforated like a colander. The locals hated the government telling them to Stop.

Mandi shook her head. She hoped this particular graffiti hadn't been done by the guys on the team as they passed by on their way to the party. But deep inside she was almost sure it probably had been. She didn't say anything to break the silence that had settled inside the SUV. Maybe it had been a mistake to take Danny after all. Certainly his presence had stifled the playful banter they were used to engaging in while on road trips.

She began circling around to the far side of the lake, following the shady winding lanes, and now Mandi was keeping her eyes peeled for the side road that would lead to Jason's parents' house.

In the end it wasn't all that hard to find.

The driveway—which *was* hidden along a huge expanse of seemingly impenetrable forest—was marked with a clump of multi-colored helium balloons and a huge hand-lettered sign: *Party Here!*

"Well, here we are," Anna the navigator announced as

Mandi pulled onto the gravel turn-in. "Made it!"

"Yeah, thanks a lot." Mandi glanced in her rearview mirror. Danny was squirming nervously while Krystal leaned forward to look through the windshield. He *might* have been staring at her side-boob.

The path was only wide enough for a single car, and massive trees crowded out the sunlight on either side of them.

"Wow, this is beautiful," Mandi said, as she let the vehicle roll slowly down the twisty lane.

"I guess," Anna said. "If you're into this kind of thing."

"I'm into partying, if that's what you mean," Krystal said.

The driveway seemed to go on forever and Mandi was just about to comment on it when the house appeared.

House?

No way, it wasn't just a normal, everyday house. It was more like a...a *lodge* than a house. A lodge *mansion*. A huge, long two-story log home with a deck that wrapped around at least two sides as far as Mandi could see. And massive floor to ceiling windows that looked out into the surrounding forest. At least one additional wing extended diagonally from the rear of the house with a flat roof that seemed to be home to some sort of rooftop garden-slash-patio. Mandi wasn't too surprised. She'd heard Tyler and Jason talking about the place, and she knew that Jason's dad was some kind of bazillionaire.

About a dozen cars had already arrived and some other partygoers were unloading their camping gear and coolers. A couple of shirtless hunks were tossing a Frisbee back and forth in a small clearing. Mandi thought their names were Dean and Mike, but she wasn't sure. A few of the other guys from the team were throwing a football, but Mandi didn't know who they were.

They pulled the Nissan up on the lawn, parallel to the other cars. There were Porsches, Alfas, a Maserati, several BMWs, more than a couple Escalades, and a variety of other exotic iron, including a Bentley and an Aston-Martin. The Nissan looked positively pedestrian next to them. Mandi popped the hatch open and slid out, pausing to arch her back in a cat-like stretch before looping around to the back of the vehicle.

"Thank God! People! And not weird!" Krystal squealed as she took in the scenery. "Not weird at all."

"Help me, don't just stand there!"

"Sure, sure, order me around." Krystal protested, but she bent over to help Mandi unload, groaning the whole time.

And then Danny and Anna were there too, throwing backpacks over their shoulders, carrying rolled sleeping bags and shuffling toward the door. Finally, Mandi and Krystal each took one side of the cooler and hauled it out of the SUV just before Mandi slammed shut the rear door.

"Hey, guys!" It was Jason greeting them, having shown up seemingly out of nowhere. His wavy black hair was cropped short, and his skin was a deep coppery bronze that came close to Anna's tanned perfection. His lean muscles bulged through his tight t-shirt.

Anna slipped her shades down onto her nose and eyed Jason up and down. She smiled widely.

"Hey, Jason," Mandi said, smirking.

Jason's own smile was brilliant. "You need a hand carrying your stuff?"

"Nah," said Mandi, but Krystal and Anna both handed Jason their sleeping bags.

"And..." Jason's voice just hung in the air for a few moments. "Danny?" He'd spotted the quiet young man and frowned.

"Oh, yeah," Mandi said, feigning nonchalant innocence. "I invited Danny to the *team* party."

"Well, yes...of course you did. Hey Danny, how's it going?"

Danny nodded. Mandi was sure he'd caught Jason's annoyed tone. Jason would just have to deal. It wasn't like she was going to turn around and bring Danny back to town.

A change of subject was in order. "Is Tyler here?"

"He's out picking up the barrel. They should be back soon." Jason turned, a sleeping bag tucked under each arm, and motioned with his head. "Let's drop your stuff off at the house and I'll show you around."

Mandi, the other girls, and Danny followed Jason, lugging the rest of their bags and camping gear.

The weather was just about perfect. The late afternoon sun had fallen behind the trees, dappling the scenery in cool shadows. And though she couldn't see it, Mandi could smell the scent of the nearby lake carried on a gentle breeze.

Mandi flinched as an errant football barely missed her head. "Hey!" Krystal yelled at the guys throwing the ball.

One ran over to claim the ball. "Sorry," he said. "Welcome to Killer Lake." He tossed the ball back to his friends.

"Killer Lake?" said Mandi, thinking of the sign they had passed. And what the old man at the gas station had said. *Be careful of the lake.*

"Oh," Jason explained, shrugging, "the guys just call it that. You know, *killer* like in *awesome, dude!*" He said, doing his best surfer imitation.

"Uh huh," Mandi nodded, unconvinced. "Okay."

"They're just goofing off, Mandi," he said, apparently sensing her unease. "Somebody crossed the letters off the signs down by the beach and it just stuck."

"It's kind of creepy. Reminds me of those movies with the serial killer.... Camp Crystal Lake or something," Mandi said. She could have sworn his appeasing tone wasn't making it up to his eyes, which held hers in a hard, unyielding stare. *As if he's pissed off I'm upset.*

"Krystal Lake?" said Krystal, grinning. "I like that."

"Sounds like your porn star name, Krystal," Anna said. "Although *Krystal Geyser* might be better!"

"Hey, fuck you!" Krystal shouted, laughing. She mimed slapping her mouthy friend.

Jason ignored them and climbed the stairs to the porch, then unceremoniously dumped the sleeping bags at his feet. "Just leave your stuff here for now. I'll show you around the house," he said, almost as if forcing himself to be polite again.

"Do you have a bathroom?" Anna said, reminding everyone they'd been in dire need of one not so long ago.

"Believe it or not we do!" Jason replied, sarcasm dripping from his words. "Complete with running water and everything, all the latest fads." He pulled open the fancy screen door that led into the house and waved them in with a smirking flourish, staring at Danny as he passed through the doorway.

Once their hands were emptied of camping equipment, Danny stealthily took Mandi's hand in his. Mandi was about to pull away instinctively when she looked up and into his face. He wasn't even really looking at her. He'd taken her hand like a child grips its mother for comfort, more or less subconsciously, she thought. Mandi smiled to herself as she watched Danny's eyes scanning the cabin with both terror and wonder in equal measure. *Poor kid. He's just out of his depth.*

Inside, the log house was opulent. In what Mandi assumed was the main living area, a tall cathedral ceiling soared way up above them. Below, huge intricately-patterned throw rugs covered portions of the hardwood floors, while naked wood portions reflected every light source as if they were coated in glass. Oversized, plush leather furniture dominated the room. The largest of several rustic sofas faced a massive two-story fieldstone fireplace in which a low fire crackled in preparation for the chilly night ahead. On the mantel a series of expensive-looking crystal art pieces had been lined up. One of the conversation pits was arranged around a huge black flatscreen mounted on the wall, surrounded by shelves of high-end vacuum-tube powered stereo components. Above them a second floor balcony overlooked the great room, a series of bedroom doors lined up across its landing. Occasional splashes of color that were abstract paintings seemed to clash with the decor, but really didn't. Mandi knew art, she'd studied it in school. Here was a Picasso, there was a Jackson Pollock. A Mondrian was under the balcony. She walked up to one... the Picasso. It wasn't a print. And it was signed.

Could it be?

Wait a minute, I think they're real!

Holy shit, if they're real then they're worth...millions!

She almost felt dizzy looking up at the bizarre portrait, the body parts suddenly looking like a serial killer's dismembered victim.

What the hell am I thinking?

She stepped back and reassessed her first impressions. Maybe it was a commissioned fake? She just didn't think so.

Nope, it's still pretty impressive.

The only thing that detracted from the room's tasteful decor—in Mandi's eyes—was the myriad of hunting trophies that hung side by side, high on the walls.

Trophies my ass, she thought.

They were heads. They were the heads of wonderful, beautiful animal life that had been murdered by someone with no cause to care about conservation or compassion. And they weren't just local species, although there were various deer and bears and other fierce-looking critters, but also all manner of exotic creature: lion, polar bear, ibex, elk, moose, and warthog heads were interspersed with the more regional game. *Disgusting,* thought Mandi. She couldn't help it, she envisioned a family of men pretending to be great white hunters, killing everything in sight just because they could. She realized she felt almost nauseated by the display of callous uncaring.

"Jason!" The deep voice boomed from somewhere else in the house, and she realized there were several hallways both below the balcony and on the balcony, all of them signaling entirely new wings to explore. Photographs mounted in expensive frames lined every hallway she could glimpse. All eyes searched for the source of the voice, and an instant later the voice's owner himself turned into the room from one of the mysterious other tunnels. It was an older man, though the voice seemed to belong to a younger one.

Must be Jason's dad.

He was impressive: tall, erect, maybe imperious. And there was something else about him... something *exciting*. He had a full head of salt and pepper hair and sported a grey soul patch on his strong chin. *He has a Kirk Douglas chin*, Mandi's dad would have said. The older man's features were chiseled, as were the age lines that spread from the corners of his eyes and mouth. And his eyes were dark and mesmerizing. He was *sexy*. With a kind of magnetic presence that ruled the room. And he made Mandi feel like putty even though he was so...*old*.

"Who are your friends, Jason?" the man asked as he approached them, his eyes roving over Mandi and the other girls. Mandi didn't mind his gaze. *Not one bit.* In fact, she tingled. Maybe even worse than just tingling...

"Oh, this is Mandi, Krystal, Anna, and...and Danny. Guys, this is my dad."

"Pleased to meet you all," Sebastian Carruthers said. The words dripped off his tongue with a politician's sensuality. *Politician, or salesman. Or both.*

Mandi and the other girls seemed to lose their voices

and murmured inaudible greetings, while Danny presented his shaky hand.

Mr. Carruthers squeezed Danny's hand tightly. "Danny...?" he asked, fishing for a last name. A look crossed over the elder Carruthers's face that Mandi couldn't quite put her finger on.

"Danny Wallace, s-s-sir."

Carruthers's gaze slid down and he eyed Danny's other hand—the one clutching Mandi's—thoughtfully.

Mandi almost wanted to pull away so he wouldn't think she and Danny were together, but the feeling passed almost immediately. It was replaced with a jab of guilt.

Who am I? God, could she have actually not wanted the old man to think they were an item? Danny was probably used to people looking at him *differently... judging him.* Mandi didn't want to be one of those people. She gave Danny's hand a little squeeze.

The elder Carruthers dismissed them with a look. "Jason, I just wanted to tell you that your mother isn't feeling well and you should keep your friends away from her wing if you can. The rest of the property is here for you to enjoy for the weekend. Just let your mother rest."

"Yeah, okay dad."

Jesus, Mrs. Carruthers has her own wing?

"Nice meeting you all," Sebastian Carruthers said with a curt nod. "I hope you'll all have a good time." Then he stalked away and disappeared in the direction from which he had arrived, his footsteps echoing down a long hallway. This house was even more massive than it had appeared to be at first.

Krystal turned to Mandi, her eyes wide, and mouthed, "He's hot!"

Mandi shook her head, but deep down she knew she agreed with Krystal. Anna seemed star-struck, too. Only Danny seemed troubled. Mandi found herself with a foot in each camp: she thought he was definitely handsome for his age, and, sure, sexy…but it also somehow troubled her that she felt that way.

She was embarrassed to feel moisture in her panties. She blushed and hoped no one noticed the quick flush of heat she knew would bloom on her cheeks.

"Come on," Jason said, almost as curt as his father had been.

Now they followed Jason down one of the halls, intricately inlaid wooden slat ceiling above them, tiny hidden spotlights aimed at wild animal art on the walls, and then through the gigantic restaurant-quality kitchen with both butcher-block islands and granite countertops and enough stainless steel appliances to look like… like the set of *Iron Chef.*

All it needs is the melodramatic music.

"The main guest bathroom is down this hall, on the left," Jason announced. "Memorize the location so you won't get lost going there." All three girls headed for it, mostly just to *see* it!

Mandi guiltily pulled away from Danny's death grip, his puppy eyes pleading with her to hurry back.

As she had expected, Mandi found this guest bathroom as exquisite as the other rooms they had seen so far. Its floor and lower walls were set with black and white tile, in a style change from the rest of the house. The upper half of the room's walls were mirrored so the room seemed endless. There were two double sink vanities set into a long black countertop of what Mandi thought was black granite, and on the other side of the room—set into the corner wall—was a whirlpool tub big enough that the three girls could have sat in it with a few more friends, a large tankless toilet set into its own private enclosure—with next to it a bidet!—and a gray-tiled, glass-enclosed shower with a dozen gleaming body shower jet heads and a manhole-size rainfall shower head above. Mandi estimated that eight people could scrub themselves clean in there simultaneously. And women could flush their privates in peace, she though, almost giggling.

So this is what money can do. Decadent. But nice... damn nice.

Krystal quickly claimed the toilet and sat down, groaning as her bladder emptied in a rush. The girls had known each other so long and shared everything along the way, so the time for self-consciousness was long past. She flushed by waving her hand over a sensor, chuckling. Then Anna and Mandi took their turns. They all rolled their eyes at the bidet.

"I definitely want to try that," said Anna.

"Me too!" Krystal nodded, blushing.

"Me not so much," Mandi offered. "But you can."

The three gathered in front of the mirror over the multiple sinks and washed their hands, then made sure they looked okay after the long drive, touching up their lips like models behind the scenes at a fashion show, helping each other play up their features.

"Wow," Krystal said, "Jason's dad is looking *good.* That's what I call a man."

"Yeah, an *old* man!" Anna pointed out.

"A *rich,* hot old man," Krystal corrected.

"A married, rich, hot old man," added Mandi.

"Yeah, well he's probably ready to trade the Mrs. in for the latest model," Krystal said, admiring her own face and curves in the mirror, pouting and winking. "Hell, he might never find her again in *her wing!*"

"Krystal! You're terrible!" Mandi said, rolling her eyes.

"Actually, I'm wonderful. At least that's what they all tell me. Young and old."

"Not half as wonderful as me," Anna said with a wink.

"Is it gonna be a contest then?" Mandi asked. "You guys here to compete in how trashy you can be?"

"Nah," Anna said. "Krystal can have the old codger. I want one who's rich *and* young."

Mandi said, "If you play your cards right you can probably have them both at the same time, young *and* old. And rich."

Mandi was shocked at what she'd just said and blushed again.

They all broke out into nervous laughter, but avoided each other's eyes.

Then the three women headed out the door, still chuckling nervously. After a seemingly long hike they joined Jason and Danny back in the hangar-sized kitchen.

"You've got a hell of a spread here, Jason," said Krystal, running her finger across the edge of an expensive countertop, one of a half-dozen. "I could really cook up something special in here."

"You cook?" Mandi said.

"Oh, no, not food...I was thinking about something *else*." Krystal grinned sinfully. "These countertops are like a challenge."

"It's getting kind of hot in here now," said Jason, color rising in his cheeks. "We should go out and get your tents set up."

"You don't happen to have a spare bed?" Krystal asked. "Or spare wing?" She playfully bit the tip of her finger, feigning innocence like an expert.

"Maybe." Jason shrugged and then winked, and they headed back through the great room and out of the house. "There's more house for you to see, but it can wait."

What does that wink mean? Mandi wondered.

Jason pointed to a clearing near all the parked cars, where the boys were still tossing the Frisbee and football around and where several small tents were already erected. "You can camp right there," he said.

But he winked again.

INSTANT
REPLAY

CHAPTER FIVE

Killdeer Lake
1993

As the strange charged cloud crept slowly through the ranks of blood-covered and naked cultists, pulses of supernatural light painted its billowing form. Though the cloud was luminous—lighting the previously absolute darkness of the ritual chamber—it was dense enough to hide the coven members from each other, giving each the sensation of total isolation. As if they were alone with their Dark Lord.

The Beast stood facing the sacrificial altar, pure evil flowing around him. He grinned widely as the concentrated energy of his omnipresent Master tickled his flesh, making the hairs rise on every inch of his exposed skin. He shuddered with ecstasy, his eyes rolling up as the pleasure rolled through him.

The fog amassed over the bloody corpse of their "lamb" and then began seeping into her every orifice—mouth, nose, ears, tear ducts, vagina, anus, and even the many gaping dagger wounds. It crept into her every pore until the entire cloud had disappeared into her body and the room was once again plunged into an enveloping darkness.

With a thunderclap all the torches set in the walls throughout the chamber re-ignited at once, burning white hot at first—nearly blinding the cultists with their intensity—and then dimming back down to cool blue flames.

Then the beautiful corpse on the altar *twitched.*

The Beast struggled to contain his glee, his toothy grin spreading over excited features. He took a deep breath and waited for this new manifestation to fully resolve.

The prior sacrificial offering jerked spasmodically in a series of stop-motion movements of her limbs, eventually working its way into a stiff and awkward sitting position.

The animated corpse sat in that position for what seemed like several lifetimes to the Beast, who waited breathlessly for the final stage of his Dark Lord's arrival. Her head was cocked to one side, her long raven hair—now stained crimson from her own blood—clinging wetly to her face. Her breasts and abdomen were painted with splashed gore, a grotesque Pollock.

The corpse's eyes snapped wide open, showing only the pupil-less milky whites.

"Master," the Beast said, the slightest tremor audible in his voice.

But he was sure the obscene chaos raging around him in the chamber disguised the sound of his nerves. Moaning in both pain and pleasure, his coven was now out of control, feeding into the energy of the visitation, and taking sexual energy back in turn. Encounters were longer, harder, more intense for all celebrating parties, and the releases were more voluminous, spilling like fountains on faces and buttocks.

"We have summoned you to offer our services to you in life and in death. We ask for nothing in return save the tools to best do your bidding. Accept this humble offering as an initial token of our servitude."

At first the vessel that held the soul of Asmodeus sat motionless and slack-jawed, white eyes staring into oblivion. But then, as if the Beast's speech had been a radio transmission from another planet—leaving a momentary silence as it traversed time and space—the lamb's occupant eventually seemed to hear, and it shifted its empty gaze toward the Beast. The corpse didn't speak but instead dragged two fingers of its right hand across its bloody abdomen, and then used them to trace symbols on a mostly unblemished portion of the altar in thick, sticky crimson.

The symbols were from no known language, but the Beast was certain he recognized them from some of the most arcane tomes in his secret library. The repository was of books that had come to him through inheritance, appropriation, or furtiveness. Several through murder, though by necessity. He traced the line of symbols silently and understood their message.

The coven's offer of servitude had been accepted by the demon.

The Beast sliced open the tip of his finger with the soiled dagger's blade and stepped forward, adding his own glyphs to the altar's surface. Thus he sealed their unspoken pact.

The vital bargain struck, the alien life force blinked out of the woman and her corpse tumbled backward like a tree trunk and sprawled on the altar with the dull *thud* of butchered meat landing on a marble slab.

The Beast looked down on her with some small amount of pity. Even in death she was beautiful—*had been* beautiful. He had loved her once, hadn't he?

And what of the child…

INSTANT
REPLAY OVER

CHAPTER

SIX

Mandi sat cross-legged in the grass near her tent, sipping from a bottled Bud she'd rescued from its watery ice-bath in the cooler. Nearby Krystal and Anna did likewise, while Danny watched the growing crowd of party-goers nervously, chewing a fingernail and ignoring his own beer.

Setting up the tent on the sunny knoll had held her attention, but now that they were done her mind returned to thoughts of Tyler. *Where is he? The nearest town couldn't be that far away!* She tried to distract herself, concentrating on the warmth of the slowly setting sun on her face and listening to Krystal and Anna's comical banter. But she couldn't deny the lift she got when she heard the approaching grumble of Tyler's Harley.

She played it cool, trying not to seem too eager, but when Tyler rolled into view she stood and half-ran over to greet him in spite of herself.

A dual-axled pick-up followed the motorcycle closely. Mandi could see their friend Marlon and a couple others sitting in the truck's bed, apparently there to safeguard the half-barrel.

Tyler dismounted. "Hey babe!" The flames on his tank reached up like hellfire.

He had barely finished forming the words when Mandi stretched up on tip-toes to taste his lips.

"I'm glad to see you too," he said when she let him pull away, wrapping her in his leather- clad arms.

"Mmmmm," Mandi purred in his ear. She loved the feel

of his day-old scruffiness against her cheek.

"Hey, are you gonna help us get this out of the truck?" Marlon whined at Tyler.

"Nope," he replied before kissing Mandi's forehead. "You guys can handle it."

Mandi cast a glance at Marlon, whose face suddenly seemed disgusted. Now she recognized the other guys on the truck, Rob and Greg—Marlon's minions, she used to call them. She raised her eyebrows and gave them a rueful smile. Her man had his priorities straight.

"Danny?" said Tyler.

Mandi turned to find Danny standing right behind her. She laughed nervously. He had followed right behind her the way a duckling follows its mother, sidling up without her even noticing.

Danny nodded by way of an answer. His discomfort was palpable.

Tyler's eyes narrowed, his brow rising. His question was obvious, though he left it unspoken: What was Danny doing here?

Mandi was about to respond, but her words caught on the tip of her tongue and she hesitated.

"Danny!" a shout came from the direction of the truck. It was Rob. And he seemed sincerely excited to see Danny. He long-stepped over and slapped Danny's shoulder in a friendly way. "It's so awesome that you came!" Danny smiled and nodded.

Maybe this wasn't going to be a disaster after all, Mandi thought. She sighed in relief. She was worrying too much. Danny *was* a member of the team, even if some of the guys didn't act like it. In fact were downright jerks about it.

Jason appeared, materializing from the growing throng of party-goers starting to loiter in cliques. He strutted over and he and Tyler high-fived enthusiastically. Jason looked over their small group. "You guys wanna tour of the grounds?"

"Hell yes," Tyler said.

Anna and Krystal nodded eagerly.

"I guess…" said Mandi. She was torn between wanting to be alone with Tyler and feeling like she should be watching over Danny.

"Well, let's go then," Jason said making a come-on motion with his hand as if leading a museum tour.

They followed, Krystal and Anna close behind Jason, Mandi behind them with Tyler's arm draped over her shoulder.

Walking backwards, Jason turned to speak, but stopped in his tracks. "No," he said sharply. "Not you!"

Mandi turned and saw that Danny had started trailing them shyly. "Oh come on, Jason," she said, "why not?"

"No, not him," Jason reiterated, pointing at Danny who squirmed under everyone's sudden scrutiny. "I didn't invite him."

Mandi felt her temper rearing up. She was just about to unleash it on Jason when Rob intervened.

"Hey Danny," Rob said. "Why don't you come with us?"

Behind Rob, Marlon was pushing the barrel on a furniture dolly. Mandi saw him roll his eyes theatrically at Rob's suggestion and shook her head as she realized how many of these people were complete assholes.

"Where do you want the beer, Jason?" Marlon asked, probably trying to change the subject in hopes that Danny wouldn't respond either way.

"There's a clearing with a firepit just past those trees," Jason said, pointing. "Follow the path."

Marlon nodded and made a course correction, cutting a path over the lawn with Greg and another broad-shouldered teammate in tow.

"Come on, Danny," Rob pleaded. "It'll be fun."

Danny looked over his shoulder at Mandi, a questioning look on his face.

She thought he'd be better off with Rob for now, especially if Jason and the others were going to have such a bad disposition toward him. She said, "Go with Rob, Danny. I'll be back in a little bit." She smiled encouragingly, hoping he would take her suggestion without making a scene. It wasn't fair, but she wasn't sure how to change Jason's mind, so this was easier.

Danny hung his head and did as she said, and guilt stabbed at Mandi as she watched him shuffling away. But Rob waved her off, seeming happy to be in Danny's company. And Tyler pulled her away.

They walked through the growing horde of partiers, many of them shouting greetings at their teammates, Jason and Tyler. Mandi felt anonymous to most of them, garnering more lustful stares than anything else. Most of the players were just pigs. Except for Tyler, and maybe Rob— she hadn't really noticed him much before but the way he handled Danny was telling.

She caught up to the rest of the gang and it felt good to have Tyler's hand in hers again.

When they came to the lawn's edge, Jason led them to a narrow gravel path that cut between the thickening clump of trees.

Mandi looked to her left, past Tyler, and beyond the tree branches she could see a field of shimmering blue. "Is that the lake?" she asked.

"Yep, that's her," Jason said. "First stop is the boathouse."

"I heard you had a boat," said Krystal. "A fast one."

"Yes, we do. A couple, actually."

"Can we go for a ride?" Anna cooed.

"Tomorrow we can take one out and maybe go water skiing, but tonight I have a party to throw."

"We could have a private party on the boat," Krystal suggested slyly. "Those are more fun anyway."

"I agree," Jason said, blushing despite his devilish grin.

"Come on you two, give him a break," said Mandi.

"Hey, leave us alone. You've already got yours," Krystal said.

"Yeah," Anna agreed, winking.

"You got that right," said Tyler, and squeezed Mandi around the waist.

They laughed and the moment was over.

The path veered to the left and when they rounded the turn Mandi could see the lake clearly, gently rippling blue water reflecting what remained of the sun's light. Off to their left, what looked like a miniature log cabin with a deck on its rectangular roof squatted over the water's edge.

"Well," said Jason, "there's the boathouse."

"Is it in there?" asked Krystal. "The boat."

"Boats," Anna corrected. Then, almost in unison, the two of them said, "Can we see them?"

"No, no. The boats aren't in there. They're over there," Jason said, pointing to the new wooden pier that stretched out into the water on the opposite side of the boathouse. A blue and white speedboat was moored on one side, bobbing gently in the lake. It looked brand new and reminded Mandi of a prehistoric stone spearhead, sharp and lethal. On the other side of the pier was a much slower looking but posh pontoon boat with a huge outboard motor mounted on the rear.

"Wow, look at that," Krystal admired the low-slung, fast-looking one. She went ahead down the gravel path to the pier, Anna bouncing close behind her.

In the short while it took for Mandi and Tyler to reach the pier, Anna and Krystal were no longer concerned with the boat. Instead, they were talking to the three football players who were swimming and splashing around nearby.

"Come on! Come in!" a running-back named Kevin called out as he treaded water on his back, giving them a partial view of his exceptional physique. "The water's great!" He winked.

"And so are we," one of the others added. He was Andy, the center.

"Hell, you even have your suit on," said the third player, Mark, the team's punter. He directed his comment to Anna who had had already stripped down to her hot red strapless bikini top.

"Not right now," Anna called back. "We're taking the big tour!" She gave *big* the splash it deserved.

"How about you?" Andy yelled out to Krystal.

"I don't have a suit," she sang.

"We don't either," said Mark, flashing a toothy smile and not much else. Well, there was the hint of something large coming to life.

Krystal turned and faced Mandi and the others. At first Mandi thought she was outraged, but then she saw that her friend was grinning like the Cheshire cat.

Oh no! Krystal's on the loose...

Then Krystal made an exaggerated shrug, turned back to face the three boys, and pulled off her shirt to reveal that she was indeed braless. Hoots met her amateur burlesque act and she bowed deeply, giving them more of her. She waved the shirt around once and tossed it on the pier, then kicked off her shoes, one at a time teasingly, paused for a long beat...then shimmied out of her tight short-shorts with a series of booty bumps. The men in the water cheered and splashed cascades like fireboats in the harbor. She was wearing black panties, but they weren't much more than two wisps of lacy cloth held together by a string. With all the guys still cheering her on, she dived gracefully into Killdeer Lake. Anna laughed and clapped and Mandi gave up and joined in.

Krystal bobbed up and grabbed the edge of the pier, then shook water from her hair and swiped stray droplets off her face, fake-sputtering for sake of the show. She knew she was the center of attention and she loved it.

"How's the water, really?" Tyler asked, though it was obvious he knew and so did everyone there.

Krystal hoisted herself up and stood balanced with her hands splayed on the pier's edge, then looked down at the erect nipples on her small but athletic breasts. Gooseflesh was rising on her arms and back, but no one was looking at that. "I guess it's a little cold!"

Everybody laughed.

"You'll get used to it," Kevin said.

"We can warm it up!" added Mark.

In response Krystal shoved off backward and jumped back into the lake, splashing the three guys, and then they were all splashing each other. The three player were circling the near-naked girl like sharks, and she was reaching down into the water with both hands.

Someone out there groaned. Then there was laughter and more splashing, and the bodies bobbed ever closer until it was hard to tell who was who.

"You guys wanna see the rest of the homestead?" Jason asked the remaining guests to draw their attention, grinning ruefully. "Obviously it won't be quite as good as that, but…"

"You mean there's more!" Tyler commented, his eyes still on the cavorting Krystal and her three unfettered beaus. "I thought we just saw it *all.*"

"Yeah, let's see the rest of the place," said Anna, rolling her eyes at Tyler. Apparently Anna had decided not to join in on the watery fun.

Mandi had to drag Tyler away, his eyes still locked on Krystal's lithe form as it bobbed in and out of the water. The three teammates seemed to be playing catch with her as the ball. "Are you done?" she asked heatedly.

"Umm, what?" Tyler said. An annoyed look flashed across his features briefly. "Uh, yeah let's go."

The group made their way off the pier and back onto the well-manicured gravel path as it twisted deeper into the woods away from the water's edge. They could still hear Krystal shrieking playfully and the guys' laughter.

They don't know what they're in for, Mandi thought. Those boys were getting more than a handful. Of course, none of them would turn it down. Mandi wondered if Krystal was planning to take on all three. As far as Mandi knew, Krystal hadn't had sex with three men simultaneously, but her friend lived life as if everything was a record to break. And she'd already had the threesome, to hear her tell it. Adding one more dick to the equation was a no-brainer for Krystal. *Appropriately,* Mandi thought, then shrugged. Maybe there would be details shared later. If she had to, she would have admitted that the water-show had turned her on more than a little.

The gravel crunched under Mandi's running shoes as she caught up and they ascended a small hill. Not far ahead she could see a small building emerging from the surrounding woods.

"And here we have the tool shed," Jason announced.

"Why is it so far from the house?" Mandi asked.

"Eh, my dad didn't want it too close. Eyesore, you know."

"Reminds you of work, right?" said Anna, chuckling.

"So you have to come all the way out here when you need something?" added Tyler.

"Oh no, we don't come out here. This is for the groundskeepers."

"Oh, *the groundskeepers...*" Tyler intoned. "Your highness has *groundskeepers.*"

"Yeah, doesn't everybody?" Mandi said with a wink.

Jason shrugged. "Not my fault, I was born into it."

They walked into the shed, which was a fairly large building, about the size of a two-car garage. The biggest riding lawn mower Mandi had ever seen crouched in the rear, flanked by two tiny regular models, though they were top of the line too. Along the sides of the building were long built-in workbenches topped with large peg-boards stocked with all manner of tools, lined up nice and neatly as if by someone with OCD.

"Remind me to come here if there's ever a zombie apocalypse," said Tyler.

"If there's ever a zombie apocalypse, we have lots of guns in a cabinet back at the house," said Jason.

"What fun would that be?" Tyler asked, grinning and picking up a chainsaw from one of the benches. "I want to be Ash." Everybody chuckled.

"Jesus, what is all this stuff?" asked Anna.

"These are called *tools*, Anna," Mandi said, imitating a kindergarten teacher. "People use them to *do* things. Then, in her normal voice, "These are like hair dryers, curling irons, hair straighteners...but for men."

"Cool! And what are these?" Anna asked, pointing.

"Those are garden shears," Jason said.

"And this?"

"Cordless drill."

"This one?"

"Umm... heavy-duty gas-powered weed-whacker."

They all chuckled.

"What's that thing that looks like an extra long fire poker?" Mandi jumped in. "Is that for the fire pit?" she asked.

"No, that's called a boat hook," Jason replied. "You use it to push the boat around in the water without getting wet."

"Look, I'm the grim reaper!" said Tyler, pulling a scythe off the wall.

"*Dim creeper* is more like it," Anna said.

Jason stepped back out of the shed and into the gathering twilight. "Well, shall we continue?"

Anna followed, but Tyler said, "I think we'll stay and check this out a little more." His hands gripping Mandi's hips from behind.

"What are you talking about?" Mandi asked. She was still a little perturbed at him for staring at Krystal back at the lake.

"I have another tool I'd like to show you," said Tyler, smiling broadly.

"Oh, come on you guys," Anna said, shaking her head. Her hands were on her hips and her brassy Puerto Rican attitude glowed. "You can jump each other later."

Mandi shrugged. She was more than a little helpless in Tyler's big warm hands—like putty, really. "We'll meet you back at the party," Mandi said, before turning around and locking lips with Tyler. Seeing Krystal playing with those boys had turned her on a little, though she wouldn't have admitted it.

"Are you ready to go on?" Jason asked Anna, who stood for a moment staring at her friend incredulously.

After a moment she sighed. "I guess so," she muttered. "Lead on."

Jason winked back at them as he led her away from the shed.

Neither Mandi nor Tyler noticed.

SECOND
QUARTER

CHAPTER SEVEN

The beer run was a lot of work.

After finding the well-hidden path between the trees, Rob and Danny followed Marlon (and the barrel) and the others to the small clearing and the firepit. The centrally located pit was just a large circle with fieldstones marking its circumference and a small pile of charred wood and ash at the center. On one side of the clearing, set at a right angle, were two rustic-looking benches made from a huge split log. Behind one of the benches, at the clearing's edge, stood a large pile of firewood, probably a cord.

Marlon rocked the barrel to get the dolly out from under it, then hefted it with a grunt and dropped it into a washtub that was half-buried nearby. Then Greg and Tony stacked the bags of ice they had brought inside the tub, around the bottom of the keg.

"Did you guys remember the tapper?" Marlon asked.

"Aw shit, I left it in the truck," said Tony, throwing up his hands. "I'll go back and get it."

"Hey, grab the cups too," Greg added.

Tony nodded and left to run his errand. Greg plopped himself down on one of the benches, a paper bag in one hand.

"So, Danny…" Greg said, smirking. "What in the *world* brings you *here*? I mean, of *all* places you could be?"

"I-I-I…" Danny stammered.

"He's on the team," said Rob. "He has as much right to be here as any of us."

"Whoa, relax, champ. I was just asking him a question."

"And I was just answering it."

"He's a big boy. I think Danny can answer for himself. Can't you Danny?"

Danny looked at Rob and then down at his feet.

Greg reached into the paper bag and pulled out a pint sized bottle of Jim Beam while he spoke. "So *what* are you doing here?"

"M-M-*Mandi* invited me," Danny said, struggling.

"Mandi, huh?" Greg unscrewed the bottle cap and took a slug of bourbon. A sour expression compressed his features when he tasted the liquor, but he smacked his lips. "She's pretty hot!" He handed the bottle to Danny. "Go ahead, take a swig."

Danny took the booze from Greg's hand, but reluctantly. He held the bottle under his nose and took a whiff first, and flinched. Tasting it, his face puckered. He thought of his uncle, and what stuff like this had almost done to him. He shouldn't really try it, but it was too late. If he didn't, he'd never fit in.

Greg burst out laughing. Even Rob smiled at Danny's reaction to the bourbon's taste.

"All right!" Greg said. "You ever drink anything like that before, Danny?"

Danny shook his head and handed the bottle back to Greg as if afraid it would bite off his fingers.

Greg held up a hand. "No, no. Go ahead, have another." He grinned. "It'll loosen you right up."

Danny hesitated, but then he looked around and caved. He took another awkward sip, this one longer, before Rob took the bottle from him.

"Here," Greg said to Danny, patting the bench. "Have a seat." He winked at Rob.

Rob took a generous mouthful of bourbon and watched as Danny complied with Greg's invitation.

Marlon strolled over and reached out for the bottle. "Let me get some of that."

"So Danny," said Greg. "You like Mandy?"

Danny didn't answer. He lowered his eyes, suddenly red-faced.

"It's okay, Danny. She's cute. I would like her too," Greg said. "I would like her all night long. Long and hard."

"Yeah, no kidding," Marlon said after he swallowed.

"So do *you* like her, Danny?" Greg said, smirking.

Danny nodded. "Y-y-yes..."

"Well, you know she's Tyler's girl, right?" Greg said cruelly.

Danny looked away from Greg and then up at Rob. His eyes were pleading. But he didn't seem to know for what.

"That's enough, Greg," Rob said.

"You didn't think she invited you up here to be with you, did you Danny?" Greg pressed, ignoring Rob entirely. His mouth was twisted in a cruel crooked line. He grabbed the bottle back and slugged down more of the amber liquid.

Danny cast his gaze downward, frozen and no words and with nowhere to go.

"You did, didn't you?" Greg said with a chuckle. "Well let me tell you what you've gotta do, Danny." Greg stood up, lurching a little.

"I said that's enough," Rob repeated.

Greg waved Rob off. "Come on, Danny, get up." Danny slowly stood, slouching. His eyes wouldn't meet Greg's. "You're gonna have to fight for her, all right? So show me what you've got." He started dancing around with his fists up like a boxer in the ring.

Danny went on staring down at his feet.

"Come on, Danny, put up your dukes!" Greg punched Danny in the shoulder. Danny stumbled sideways, and Greg punched him again. *Hard.* You could see the surprise in Danny's eyes.

"Jesus, Greg! Stop!" Rob said, stepping forward.

Marlon held up his free hand to halt Rob's advance, while he tipped back the bottle to his lips with the other. Then he raised an eyebrow at Rob and mouthed the word *Watch!* He winked.

Self-consciously, Danny curled his hands into loose fists and made a half-hearted attempt to hold them up in the same way as Greg.

"Now dance around a little, Danny," said Greg. "Come on, show me your fancy footwork. Come on, if you stand still you get pounded." He feigned another punch and Danny flinched.

With a desperate look, Danny began to bounce on his feet a little.

"You're never going to take out Tyler like that," Greg goaded. "He's a pretty big guy. And tough, too. Get your hands up," he kept prodding. "Jesus, throw a couple punches!"

Danny picked up his tempo and started to look more sure of himself as he danced away from Greg's feigned punches. He looked like an amateur shadow boxer preparing to take down his imaginary opponent. But at least he was moving.

"Left, left," Greg coached. "Now a quick right!"

With a furrowed brow, Danny imitated Greg's movements.

"*Now* you've got your game face on," called out Greg, his face suddenly red. "Are you ready for Tyler?"

Danny nodded.

"Are you ready for Tyler!" Greg repeated. He was snorting through his nose now.

Danny nodded, trying to appear more adamant.

"Are you ready for Tyler!" Greg taunted again, sounding like some kind of demented athletic coach or trainer. And a locomotive, snorting in and out, his nostrils flaring. His eyes were simultaneously wide and slitted, aroused and guarded.

"*Y-y-yes!*" Danny spat out more out of fear than anything else.

"Here he comes," Greg shouted. At the same time he swung a vicious right cross, his knuckles smashing against Danny's left cheekbone.

Danny tumbled backward onto the ground, hard. His hand shot up over the left side of his face and the shock of the blow showed in his eyes. He scrambled back awkwardly, afraid of more.

Rob took three steps forward and shoved Greg's chest with both hands, taking him by surprise. He was about to raise his own fist to rearrange Greg's face when he half-turned to see Danny leap up and dart away across the clearing.

Pulling the punch so it swished past Greg, Rob turned and shouted, "Danny!"

But Danny didn't stop his flight. He half-ran, half-stumbled out of the clearing with his left hand still cupped over his battered cheek and collided with Tony, who had just returned with the cups, knocking him over before disappearing into the undergrowth.

"What the fuck are you doin'!" Rob screamed directly into Greg's face.

"Whoa, man," Greg said, smiling and holding up his hands in surrender. "I was trying to teach him something. And I thought he was going to defend himself." His smile made a liar out of him.

"Bullshit!"

"Take it easy, Rob," Marlon said. His nearby voice was soft and diplomatic to defuse the situation. "I'm sure Danny's fine. That punch of Greg's bruised his ego more than his face. He probably just went back to their tent. Let him cool off for a while. Here." He handed Rob the well-dented Beam bottle.

Rob let his breath slow and took a deep drink after

snatching the bottle. But he glared at Greg's grinning face and wanted to punch him.

At the clearing's edge, Tony was picking himself up gingerly and trying to corral cups that had spilled all over the path. He gave his friends a questioning look, then shrugged and got the rest of the cups in a pile.

"What's with him?" he called out, but no one answered. He shrugged. "Whatever."

There was no trace of Danny. He'd disappeared down the path in the direction from which they'd come.

CHAPTER EIGHT

Jason was still leading the way, with Anna following close behind. *Very close.* She was practically glued to him. He grinned to himself, but didn't let on he was aware of her closeness. He'd been hoping for a chance to get her alone, and with Tyler and Mandi dropping out of the remainder of the tour his plan was working just perfectly.

"Where are we going?" Anna's voice edged toward whining. *That* was one thing he wasn't thrilled with. "Come on, I wasn't planning on walking through the woods. I thought we were going back to the lake." As if to make her point, Anna stomped heavily through the low brush in her Birkenstock sandals, short-cut denim shorts, and bikini top, making a face the whole time. He liked what he saw.

"Just a little bit farther. This is really cool, you're gonna love it."

"Love what?"

"You'll see. We're almost there."

"I'll see? I'm not sure about that. It's getting so dark out here I can barely see now!"

"Well, if you took your shades off..." Jason said with a smirk.

"Oh, yeah." She pushed the Aviators up to rest on her head.

But actually it *was* getting dark. A few slices of magenta sky still showed overhead in the spaces between the trees, but before long it would fade to black. Anna hoped they'd be able to see well enough to get back to the house when the stupid tour was over. Then she noticed the clearing just ahead of them, barely visible through the undergrowth.

Jason parted the last stand of tallish weeds and stepped aside, displaying the open area to Anna as if he were a model on *The Price is Right.* "And...here we are," he said.

They emerged into an area that suddenly seemed oddly devoid of vegetation. It was a circular plot roughly five yards in diameter that stretched upward towards the sky, as if the trees had chosen to avoid branching out over its perimeter. The ground itself was hard-packed, parched earth with cracks running through it like the glaze on a hundred-year-old ceramic tea cup.

"What is it?" Anna came up next to him, thoroughly unimpressed. "What am I supposed to be looking at?"

"This." Jason waved at the space, then shrugged. "I guess it's just some kind of weird clearing in the woods. I dunno. It wasn't here when I was a kid, but at some time or other it just...showed up. I thought it was cool. Maybe like an alien landing pad or something."

"You brought me out here to see an alien landing pad?"

"Sorry, I thought it was interesting. After it showed up overnight, I was still a kid and I started to come out here a lot. It's...just a good place to go to get away from all the crap," Jason said as he slowly moved closer to Anna. He slipped a hand around her bare waist.

"Oh," Anna said, glancing down. "Now I see what you brought me out here for." She shoved Jason's hand away and took a small step back.

"Come on, Anna," Jason said, holding his hands out to prove he was unarmed. "That's not why we came here. I just thought you might like to see it, that's all. But now that we're out here, all alone..."

"Uh huh, sure, now that we're suddenly, surprisingly all alone..."

"Jeez, give a guy a break. It's not a big deal. We're both

young and single. Come on, Anna."

He put a hand on her waist again, caressing her smooth skin.

She took another small step back. A smaller step.

"What? What are you gonna do if I say no? Rape me?"

"God, no! I'm not gonna *rape* you. I just thought you were...*fun*. I know you, uh, slept with Zack, and Mason, and Jake Doleman. I thought you liked to have a good time."

Now he was smiling crookedly. The cadence of her breathing probably gave her away, and she suddenly found herself thinking it over. Jason was *so* good-looking. *And rich.* She could tell he seemed to think he had this in the bag. She shouldn't make it easy, though. She wasn't *that* easy. Jesus, how did he know about all those others? Was she the butt of jokes?

"I did invite you to the party," he said, clearly trying hard to drive his points home, "and I'm not talking about going all the way. I mean, I understand that's a lot of commitment, and a major life decision and all that."

She nodded agreement. This was better. Maybe he *was* perfect! Usually guys just wanted to get into her pants, but Jason was better than that. Jason seemed to understand her and to take her point of view seriously. Maybe he just wanted to make out, and she wasn't against that at all.

And then he said: "How about just a quick blow job? I won't tell anyone."

No! Damn it all, he's no different than the rest of the guys on the team!

She shook her head. She should let him have it. She made a fist and thumped the outside of her thigh.

But he's so cute. And rich. And so cute.

It was like a video on repeat. And she slid her gaze down from his lovely face and his movie-star smile, down his gorgeous chest and pecs and his abs and the slight curve of his waist where it disappeared into his pants… And she thought of him below that, and she imagined what it would be like. She licked her lips. He was staring, breathing hard.

She hesitated, shaking her head again. Then she sighed. "I can't believe I'm doing this."

And she got down on her knees.

CHAPTER NINE

Jason had started to harden just thinking of Anna's sweet lips. Now her beautiful face was even with him, and he was bursting. She reached out and massaged the stiffening through his jeans, then undid his zipper and wrestled him out through the slit in his briefs, stroking him all the while.

She's done this before.

Then his coherent thinking shut down.

Jason's breathing quickened as he watched her take him slowly into her mouth. The warm, wet touch of her tongue and lips made him momentarily lightheaded and his knees threatened to buckle under him in a rush of pleasure. He gasped, choking down air in gulps. His heart pounded like a heavy metal double kick-drum.

"Oh yeah, baby," he whispered unconsciously, as Anna started sliding up and down on him, bobbing her head and increasing her pace. Jason began thrusting his hips in rhythm with her movements, tuning into the moaning sounds she was making and reaching out for ecstasy that was just around the corner. "Oh, baby…"

But suddenly she released him and pulled away abruptly. The warmth on his flesh was replaced by quick cold.

Just like that!

Oh no, no, noooo!

Who does that to a guy this late in the game?

He wanted to double over in pain and frustration.

Jason started to complain, but at the same time he sensed that something strange had happened. He could have sworn that when Anna stopped what she was doing to him, the trees hemming them in had *flinched*. But that had to be his imagination...

"Oh, my God!" Anna shrieked.

And then he realized that she hadn't moved away from him at all...No, she'd *fallen* away as a section of the clearing's center collapsed, forming a jagged pit about six feet across and four feet deep. She must have been standing on a ledge or something, since he could still see her but she was below him.

"Jesus, are you all right?" Jason held out his hand. He didn't seem to be so far from the edge of the hole himself, so he backed up a little.

Anna grabbed Jason's outstretched hand and little by little he was able to wrench her up from the hole, helping her place her feet carefully and climb.

"What the hell?" Anna said, shaking her head as she stepped onto the same firmer ground that he stood on. They both backed up quickly.

"Must be some kind of sinkhole. Are you okay?"

"God, I could have twisted my ankle." Anna took a couple more steps away, watching her feet. "Or worse!"

"But you're okay, right?"

"Yeah, I think so."

"Okay, good," Jason said. He cleared his throat. "Do you think you could..." He motioned down toward where she'd been busy just moments before, a bulge still in evidence. Apparently his erection had survived the sudden scare. He reached out for her arm to help lower her back down.

"God, you are such an asshole!" Anna yelled, slapping Jason's hand away. "Fuck you!" She gave him the finger before storming off into the now completely darkened woods.

"Anna! If you would just finish what you started, that would be fine," Jason called out after her. Not whining at all—well, in truth he knew he was whining a little—but she had already strutted away, disappearing into the leafy dark shadows.

He waited for her to come back. She *had* to come back. *Right?*

"Damn it." Jason sighed and looked down at his throbbing bulge. "I guess it's just you and me, big guy..." He reached down and began rubbing himself, seeking release from the condition in which Anna (*the bitch!*) had left him.

He closed his eyes and as he stroked he tried to picture Anna's head gliding up and down on him. Her wet mouth. Her eyes looking up at him. With some effort, he neared the happy moment. Completely uncaring that he was mauling his own flesh in the middle of the woods and near a damn sinkhole.

Then *something* grasped him by the ankle from behind.

Jason looked down and tried to see what the hell was going on. But before he could put together a reasonable picture, whatever had grabbed hold of his leg tugged it out from under him and he fell face-first onto the ground. Fortunately, his free hand swept up and involuntarily protected his face from the brunt of the fall. His other hand moved to cup his groin instinctively.

"What the fuck!"

Jason rolled on his back, ready to fight, ready to smack somebody for this stupid joke. But his leg was still tightly held by someone or something he couldn't quite see. He managed to twist his trouser leg around. His protected (but quickly shriveling) manhood momentarily forgotten, he propped himself up on his elbows to figure out what was holding him down. Around his leg was what looked like a lump of *something*...Maybe dirt? But how could *dirt* hold him so tightly?

The fact that the full dark of night had settled in didn't make it any easier for him to decipher the particulars of his situation. All he really knew was that he was lying prone next to a sinkhole with something wrapped around his *fucking* leg! And that he'd been interrupted twice from getting off. That *really* sucked.

Though his eyes had somewhat adjusted, Jason fleetingly wished he'd brought a flashlight.

But who packs a flashlight when trying to get blown by a hot chick, even if it was in the fucking woods?

He tried to reposition himself so he could get his face closer to whatever it was, and managed to twist his body enough to do it. He could see better now. Something trailed off the lump that seemed to be holding him fast, and as Jason studied it he realized that it was like an arm connecting to a person—or really some kind of human shape—that was standing inside the sinkhole crater.

Inside the sinkhole?

Whatever the fuck it was, it stood a still as a statue. Maybe its face was turned toward him, but he couldn't be sure. Maybe he was hallucinating the whole thing.

Anna's blowjobs had been known to cause blackouts, he had heard (and tonight he'd wanted to find out for himself), but this was going too far.

Jason felt the grip on his leg tightening...*maybe*. His imagination? He tried to pull away, but the figure still held him tight. But was it tighter? He kicked at the mitten-like lump of a hand, if that was what it was, and when he did... *the figure came to life*.

"Jesus!" he shouted, surprised.

Then the thing's *second* appendage swung down on his genitals with the force of a sledgehammer.

Jason gasped.

The blow was so painful that it sucked all the air out of Jason's lungs, and the scream that escaped his mouth was no scream at all, but more like an asthmatic's wheeze drawn out to a tortured whimper.

Jason had the fleeting thought that he had no idea he could feel so much pain, that there could be so much pain in the entire universe. In fact the pain was all he could think about, as all other brain functions had shut off and simply acted as sensors for the finely-tuned agony that screamed through his nerves and threatened to make his head explode.

Then the shape, which was barely human after all, grasped Jason's crushed genitals in one cold mitt and his head in the other...

And pulled him into the pit.

And then there was even more pain, excruciating pain, but he was beyond feeling it very quickly.

CHAPTER TEN

Mandi was distracted.

Though Tyler was rather skillfully running his tongue around her engorged sex in tight little circles, she was having trouble relaxing and enjoying it.

And after all the time it had taken to train him!

But her mind wasn't in the right place.

For one thing, they'd decided to fool around in the tool shed. They had necked for what seemed like a long time, then after heating up and letting their hands do some wandering over each other's bodies, they had looked around for a way to go farther but the place wasn't really conducive to romantic tussling. Mandi was all for spontaneity, but she was also committed to cleanliness and sanitary conditions (maybe all the way to the level of obsessive, she thought now, but still…). Bless his little bad-boy heart, Tyler had understood her obsession and gone out of his way to make her a bed of sorts using their discarded clothes, but it didn't help overcome the gritty concrete floor, which was entirely unyielding, scratching Mandi's bare flesh where she'd slipped off the piled-up clothes. Well, she hadn't only slipped off, but she'd been shoved across a few inches of jagged little rubble bits that embedded themselves into the soft parts of her buttcheeks.

And secondly, Tyler had insisted they leave the shed's door wide open. Knowing him, the bad boy again, probably for the added thrill of potentially being caught in the act. But for Mandi that was more of a concern than a thrill.

Considering how dark it had gotten, they were more likely to get tripped over than spotted doing it in the shed by anyone who happened upon them.

Mandi sighed and tried hard to focus on Tyler's talented tongue. She forced her pelvis up and ground her hips against his face. His hands had worked their way back up her body and he kneaded her small but perky breasts, pinching her hard nipples between finger and thumb. While her body reached for orgasm, she knew that if she didn't achieve it she would just fake it so she could get back to the house and shower. But she was starting to get there, pushing the details of the situation out of her mind, and bearing down harder on him with her secret places. Places he knew well.

Moaning as she approached the plateau, Mandi gripped the back of Tyler's head and forced him hard against her. She was panting, her eyes squeezed shut, awaiting the elusive sweet release and starting to feel it. She encouraged him with a stronger grip and that hitchy grunting sound that seemed to come from deep down in her throat and that he always laughed at her about afterward.

He was so good, though, that all thoughts of the tiny jagged rocks beneath her were but a memory.

Suddenly Tyler's face slammed violently against Mandi's most sensitive spot.

"Oww!"

It was shock more than pain, but it derailed the big O-train right when it was gaining the right speed.

What the hell is he doing?

She looked down at Tyler, trying to make out his shape below her in the dark shed. She squinted, as if somehow this would increase the amount of light available.

Then she did see him.

And she wished she hadn't.

His eyes were wide and staring and his gaping mouth produced ugly choking, gurgling sounds. Something warm and wet dribbled out of Tyler's open mouth and onto Mandi's abdomen, and she knew immediately that it wasn't just her sex juices left on her lover's lips.

No, she *knew* it was not.

Mandi screamed.

Tyler jerked forward once, twice, and the fluid poured out of his mouth in a great gush. Now—even in the low light—Mandi could see it was a dark, thick liquid. Instinctively she knew what it was. Mandi squirmed backwards *hard*, trying desperately to get out from under the torrent of Tyler's gruesome stream of vomit and...*and whatever*.

Then Mandi looked back along the arch of Tyler's naked back, following the curve to where his bare buttocks stuck up into the air, and someone or *something*—something vaguely human now stood behind him.

She couldn't tell in the darkness of the shed exactly who or what it was. It looked to her sort of like a person but without well-defined features, like a snowman or an unfinished clay sculpture.

And it had something in its hands. She couldn't make it out...

She was too busy panicking.

Mandi screamed and crab-walked backwards away from Tyler and whatever that other *thing* was. Even in the darkness she could clearly see the whites of Tyler's bulging eyes, staring past her and into infinity. He gurgled some words she couldn't make out, but it was obvious all the fight had gone out of him, and the words sounded something like an apology. Or a prayer.

It was all so surreal, and even though she knew she was still screaming, it was as if a part of her broke off and watched from above. It became apparent to that detached part of Mandi that the thing standing behind Tyler was holding a handle of some sort. It looked like a broomstick. And he, or *it*, was slowly thrusting the rod forward inexorably—

into Tyler. It was impossible, wasn't it? It looked like the rod or whatever it was and been thrust between the cheeks of Tyler's ass. As she watched, struggling to comprehend, Tyler's eyes bulged even more in horror and what had to be terrible pain.

Oh my God! Oh no, oh God!

The attacker was...oh God, he had to be sodomizing Tyler with whatever it was he held!

A lightning jab of pain through her brain short-circuited the knowledge of what she was seeing.

She did not want to know.

But she did.

Mandi didn't even seem to be breathing, and the screaming she heard she only vaguely realized was hers.

She was trembling uncontrollably as she watched the thing that was like an unfinished statue lift her boyfriend effortlessly off the ground like a child's puppet. It held him upright above its head with the wooden shaft, his still-living, screaming body sliding wetly down the pole until the thing's hand-like appendages stopped poor Tyler's descent with probably three feet of broomhandle crammed impossibly into his body cavity. His limbs kept twitching for a few seconds, turning him into a grotesque flesh and blood marionette.

Fight or flight instincts finally kicking in, Mandi managed to get her feet under her. She wanted to help Tyler, but what could she do, really? His eyes were wide open and staring, glazed, from what she could tell. She had to think of herself now, *had* to. Or *she* would be next. All she could do was hope the monstrous thing moved, opening up a path. It didn't seem to be paying any attention to Mandi, focusing entirely on poor, still-twitching Tyler.

Tyler, who had to be dead, didn't he? Didn't he?

Dead!

No...please don't let him be dead.

Still panicked about herself as well as what was happening to Tyler, Mandi tried to gauge what the thing was looking at, but its lack of visible eyes made it hard to tell. It was still obstructing her only escape from the shed.

Suddenly the monster-thing shook the broomhandle downward, *hard*, making Tyler's body vibrate and slide off the bloody-greasy wooden shaft in short hitches. Then it suddenly pulled the makeshift weapon from Tyler's flesh with a sickeningly wet *gushing* sound she knew she would hear for the rest of her life.

If she survived to even have a life.

Tyler's eyes seemed to explode, spewing blood and pus, and his head deflated like a party balloon.

And now Mandi could see that it wasn't just a simple broomhandle that the *thing* had used on him...*it was the boat hook*. And its wickedly barbed point must have snared Tyler's intestines, which the thing now pulled out of Tyler's corpse from behind, foot after disgusting, bloody foot.

Stifling the screams that bubbled up anew, Mandi forced herself to be clear-headed enough to know she couldn't wait any longer. Now that the disgusting thing was finishing with the broken vessel that had been Tyler, it had all the time in the world to go after Mandi without distraction.

It was literally now or never.

She just knew...

Poor Tyler was never coming back from this.

She took her chances and charged past the thing, instinctively feinting left and then swinging around on its right with plenty of room, wasting no time looking at it.

If I don't see it, it can't grab me!

When she reached the shed door, Mandi turned back to glance at what she'd left behind. She'd planned on running for her life, but a sense of duty required her to check back one last time and see if there was any way she could attempt to save Tyler.

The monster seemed to take no real notice of her, but instead continued his leisurely disemboweling of Tyler's corpse. And there was no doubt now in Mandi's mind that Tyler was dead, for he looked like blood-soaked a rag doll.

She thought her head would explode from the pressure of what she had seen and was seeing, which was so removed from her reality that she was ready to pray she would awaken in a hospital bed to learn she'd had a stroke. Anything to be able to deny what was there in front of her.

But she knew it was real. It *felt* real. It didn't feel like a hallucination, or a nightmare. Her skin burned, her brain hurt with a pressure that was like a steel belt tightening every moment.

No, it *was* real.

And it was too late for Tyler, she was sure of it.

Taking a deep breath, relieved that, at the very least, she was now no longer trapped but on the side of the thing that led to help, Mandi finally gave in and screamed once long and hard to let out her fear, confusion, and anger.

She clipped it off, surprised and horrified at what she'd done.

She hadn't planned to do it. She hadn't told herself, *good time to scream!* It just happened that when she opened her mouth to suck in a mouthful of air, her gasp just turned into a screech.

And now she was doubly horrified to see the thing drop the bloody boat hook and turn to face *her*.

CHAPTER ELEVEN

Marlon tossed another log into the fire pit. It sputtered and kicked out a plume of bright sparks. Tony was standing on the far side of the leaping flames, tapping a beer into his red Solo cup. Greg passed a joint to Rob, who waved him off with a grunt.

"Wow, what's your deal?" Greg asked Rob, whose bad attitude was palpable.

"I don't know, Greg. You're kind of a douchetard. That's my deal."

"Whoa, man. You lookin' to get your head busted?" Greg rose slowly from his seat on the rough-hewn, half-log bench both he and Rob were sitting on.

"By who, *you*?"

"Hey, hey, hold on guys," Marlon interrupted, taking the joint from Greg's hand. He sat down beside Rob and took a hit before speaking again, holding the smoke in his lungs. "Let's not get carried away here! We're all friends, right?" he squawked. Finally he exhaled a cloud.

"If he wasn't such a fucking asswipe there wouldn't be a problem," Rob said with a smirk.

"Whoa, whoa. Is this still about the Danny thing? Because that's over, Rob. I mean *we...*" Marlon motioned toward the other guys, "...didn't really want him hanging out with us anyway. We're not babysitters. And we couldn't really be doing *this...*" he held up the joint to illustrate, "... with him around, either. Who knows who he might tell? But you know he's fine. He's probably just sitting up at the house talking to...whoever. Now just lighten up and enjoy yourself."

Tony handed Rob a cup of cold beer. "Really, Rob, I'm sure he's fine."

Rob took the beer reluctantly, but he took it.

"Where the hell is everybody else?" Greg asked.

Marlon shrugged. "I guess they're still swimming. Or back at the house. They'll be here eventually. After all, we have the beer." He raised his cup in a toast.

Rob tipped a swallow from his Solo. His heart really wasn't into it. He couldn't get the image of Greg punching Danny out of his mind. He knew Greg deserved some payback, and he was running through his head the idea of hitting Greg *hard* at the next practice. Real hard. *Payback*-hard. He considered heading back toward the house to see if he could find Danny and see how he was doing. Only a pin-dick like Greg would hit someone like Danny to try and prove some sort of masculine bullshit point. Rob had always thought that—no matter how big he was—hitting someone as timid as Danny didn't make you a *man*...it made you an asshole. And when he thought about it, he realized that he knew a *lot* of assholes. A whole lot. It made him pissy and irritable now that he was here, surrounded by them.

He was just about to get up and walk back to the house—or maybe down to the lake—when something crashed through the brush not far from their clearing. And it sounded as if it was headed their way.

"Jesus, you hear that?" Greg asked. "What the fuck is it?"

"Yeah, yeah," Marlon said, glancing around. "I hear it, but fuck if I know. You still have that flashlight, Tony?"

"Sure, hold on." Tony bent over the half-barrel, which was resting in a half-buried washtub full of ice, finally procuring a small flashlight. He turned on the powerful LED beam and aimed it into the woods. The rustling noise was definitely getting louder, but his beam was useless, not penetrating far into the tree line.

"Is that a bear, maybe?" Greg said. Nervously.

Marlon shushed him. "Just listen!"

A dark shape pushed through the undergrowth and crashed into the clearing, arms and legs swinging like windmills, and charged directly at Rob and the others as they stood ready to fight or run.

It was Mandi.

Rob felt a rush of obvious lust when he realized she was completely naked, but it evaporated quickly not only because of the hysteria in her eyes but also the blood smeared over her abdomen and legs.

The blood! Holy shit, the blood!

She ran directly to him, but it was as if she couldn't even see him and she ran *into* him and then tried to run *through* him. She almost knocked him over but he dug in and stopped her onrushing lunge.

"Mandi!" Rob yelled into her face, grabbing her by the shoulders before she could try to run him over again. "*Mandi!*"

Her eyes were wild, wide open and staring as if she'd never seen another human being in her life. Or as if she'd seen the devil himself in the woods.

And the blood, there was the blood.

Whose blood?

Not hers.

"Mandi, it's Rob. What happened? *Mandi!*"

She stared at him, struggling to speak—unable to find her voice. When he realized from the corner of his eye that Greg—actually everyone there—was ogling her, Rob pulled off his t-shirt. "Here, put this on," he said, and tried pulling it over her head.

She started to fight him off, but he grabbed her shoulders and shook her a little. "Mandi! You're naked! Here, I'm trying to get you covered up."

She sagged suddenly and allowed herself to be helped. Rob glared at his friends, just daring them to say or do anything stupid. When she was somewhat covered she said only one word: "Tyler."

"Tyler? What about him?" Rob asked. "Did he do this to you? Are you okay? Are you bleeding? *What did Tyler do?*"

Mandi let out a long sigh. She tried to regulate her breathing, her head down. She seemed to be calming. Then she raised her head and faced Rob. "Tyler's *dead.*"

"What?" Marlon said.

Rob just shook his head and kept on shaking it.

"He's d-d-dead. Somebody...some *thing.* Something killed him. It was horrible..."

"What are you talking about? What thing? An animal, or...*what?*" Marlon's voice rose in what might have been panic.

Mandi blew up. "Some fucking *thing*! I don't know! It's like a guy in some kind of fucked-up suit that looks like it's covered in dirt. It killed Tyler with a..." Her voice broke and she started to sob quietly.

Greg leaned in. "A what? A gun? We didn't hear any shots..."

"No, no..." She shook her head, unable to continue. Tears coursed down her cheeks continuously now.

"Where, Mandi? Where is it?" Rob asked calmly, trying to regain control of the situation. Whatever the situation *was.*

"Back by the tool shed is where it was, where we were, where we were just...but I think now it's following me. I think it wasn't far behind me. We should get to the house and call the police. Tyler—" She started sobbing again.

"You go back to the house, Mandi," Rob spoke quietly, but all the while his eyes scanned the surrounding trees, "We're gonna check it out."

Her red eyes widened. "No please, don't go back there! And don't leave me alone!"

"Okay, relax. Someone will go with you."

"I'll do it," Greg volunteered.

"The fuck you will," Rob barked at Greg. He looked around. "Tony, can you take her back to the house?"

"Yeah, sure." Tony handed Marlon the flashlight. Then he gingerly wrapped his arm around Mandi's shoulder.

"Fuck you," Greg spit out. But he backed off.

Rob clapped his friend on the shoulder. "You go with Tony," he told Mandi. "You'll be all right. We just want to see what we're dealing with."

Rob gave Tony a nod, and the two walked away down the path towards the distant lights that shone through the woods. Rob and the others watched until Tony and Mandi had vanished among the dancing shadows thrown by the flickering bonfire.

"Do you think she's serious?" Marlon said.

"I think she thought she's serious, but it sounds to me like someone was pulling her leg, playing some kind of sick joke on them both. Or maybe Tyler's in on it." Rob was uncertain, but it had to be something like that.

"Or maybe she's trying to mess with *us*," Greg said.

"No," said Rob. "That's not Mandi's style. She's too nice to try and pull something like that. Besides, she's not the type to go streaking through the woods without a damn good reason."

"Now that you mention it, she looked pretty damn *hot!*"

"Oh shut the fucking hell up, Greg."

Rob went to the stack of wood that had been set aside to feed the firepit. He'd noticed something before and wanted to see if it was still there. It was. Among the broken branches and narrow split logs lay a length of two-by-four, maybe about three feet long. He picked it up like a baseball bat, swung it a couple times to get the feel for it in his hands. Then, after thinking about it for a fraction of a second, he offered the wood to Marlon. "I'll trade you for the flashlight," he said. "In case she was right and something bad did happen, I'd rather have the guy with the biggest shoulders doing all the swinging."

Marlon nodded, handed over the light, and took the makeshift club in exchange.

"So which way is the tool shed?" said Greg.

"I guess it's probably that way, where Mandi came out of the woods," Rob said, motioning with the flashlight beam. He followed it out of the clearing and into the night-black forest. The others followed, muttering. He wasn't sure they believed, like he did, that something terrible had happened, but for the moment they accepted his leadership in finding out.

It quickly became apparent this wasn't going to be a stroll along the sidewalk. The woods were clogged with waist-high weeds, saplings, and other brush. Fallen tree branches littered the forest floor and low-lying, clinging vines became tripping hazards. The undergrowth tore at Rob's bare skin. He wondered how Mandi had made it through, running without a stitch of clothing to protect her. *She must have been terrified.*

Rob and the others fought their way through the tangle, but before they could start arguing about the direction— which would have been likely soon—they discovered that Mandi hadn't been lying, or joking.

Not at all.

Just a few yards into the woods their flashlight beam illuminated a figure. A shape unlike anything Rob had seen before, or expected to see now. He shined the light up and down on a bulky man-like thing that seemed to be comprised entirely of hard-packed earth. It had no defining features whatsoever: no eyes, no ears, no mouth, no clothes, and nothing that would help determine the thing's sex. At its joints most of the dirt that covered it had fallen away leaving deep fissures that seemed to go all the way through, like the joints on a wooden marionette. At the end of its right arm—which ended in a digitless hand that resembled nothing other than an oven mitt—it held an axe. The strange figure stood as still as a statue, but a thin rain of dust seemed to be continuously falling from its form, sounding like the gentle breeze rustling the leaves around them.

"What the fuck are you supposed to be?" Marlon asked the figure uncertainly.

It did not respond.

Rob eyed the axe nervously.

"Come on, Tyler. Jason, is that you? Or who the hell are you?" Greg's bravado barely masked the tremble note in his voice.

Real or fake, still the man-thing did not respond. It stood stock-still with the axe poised in its claw like the tin-man from *The Wizard of Oz*, rusted in place. But, strangely, a lot more menacing.

Marlon hefted the two-by-four like Babe Ruth in the batter's box. "You better start talking or I'm gonna knock the living shit out of you!"

"We're serious," Rob said, trying to keep himself and the others calm. But he was getting a feeling. "This isn't funny anymore."

For a few moments the young men and mud-thing engaged in a silent standoff, until Marlon couldn't take another instant. "All right, don't say I didn't warn you, fucker!" He stepped forward and swung the plank with every ounce of force his 300-plus pound frame of muscle could muster.

And he struck the thing solidly on the left side of its head, delivering a blow that should have stunned a buffalo.

But the thing was no buffalo. No, it was something else.

The thing's neck snapped to the right and a huge chunk

of the hard-packed dirt that comprised its head flew off and landed in the surrounding brush with a crunch. But the thing didn't fall. Instead, it stood for a moment with what was left of its head cocked to one side.

Rob played the light onto that damaged featureless face. The head was now only half the size it had been. The clump of dirt or whatever it was that Marlon had knocked loose with the two-by-four had exposed something… he couldn't tell, but maybe it was the yellowed bone of an old skull hiding beneath the compacted soil that caked the thing. Rob and his teammates stood silent and motionless as the sight sank into their reeling minds. Almost half of the skull was now visible. Its jawbone filled with earth, leaving it with a permanent open-mouthed grin. Its nasal aperture and eye socket stuffed with dirt. A lone skinny earthworm wiggled half-exposed where its eyeball should have been. It stood, taunting them with its very existence.

Then—with the speed of a cat and the precision of a machine—the thing flew into motion. With what seemed like no effort at all, the monstrosity returned Marlon's blow, swinging the axe with one hand and burying the blade down to the handle into Marlon's head with a sickeningly wet *thunk.*

Reacting instinctively, Rob turned and ran before the sound of Greg's scream had even registered in his mind.

There was no way Marlon had survived that. *There was no way.*

Marlon was dead. Jesus Christ, his friend was dead.

Blind terror took over control of his limbs and his mind tried to blank out the image of what he had just seen. But it couldn't, not really.

The brush that had seemed so difficult to maneuver through before was no longer an obstacle as Rob crashed through the woods towards the clearing and firepit, but his mind was trying to both process what had happened and simultaneously focusing on his car and getting into it so he could get the hell out of here at any cost. He heard Greg running beside him in the same direction, with the same total abandonment, breath coming fast and ragged.

Sharp branches and saplings sliced ruthlessly into their faces and limbs. Neither of them cared. Nothing could slow them down.

In seconds they reached the clearing. Rob hurtled the wood pile beside the bonfire on his way toward the path, just before hearing Greg trip on the same stack of timber. Greg hit the ground hard, grunting as the air was driven from his lungs. Rob slowed and turned, reaching down to help his fallen teammate back on his feet. Greg was scrambling up onto his hands and knees when Rob saw the shape materializing behind him.

Rob didn't even have enough time to shout a warning before the axe arched down, its blade biting into Greg's lower back, skewering his right kidney. Greg shrieked in pain and fear and collapsed flat on the ground. He raised his head and his bulging eyes sought out Rob's, pleading. His hand reached out, begging for help.

Rob stretched to grab Greg's hand, but before he could reach it, the thing used the axe to yank Greg backwards, dragging him across the ground by pulling on the handle with the blade still embedded in Greg's shank like a grotesque hook. Then the thing placed one encrusted foot on Greg's calf and pried out the axe head with the gross sound of skin and bones and flesh parting like those of a chicken on the butcher's block.

Rob backed off desperately and watched in helpless horror as the monster swung the blade down again, this time cleaving the crown of Greg's skull in two. A gush of blood and brain matter immediately washed out Greg's deflated features in a crimson geyser.

Rob turned and bolted toward the house, that last image burned into his retinas forever.

CHAPTER
TWELVE

The cool water had heated up very nicely when all three hunky football players started rubbing their muscular bodies on Krystal's softer curves. Krystal wasn't shy, grabbing their dicks under the murky water's surface as they swam by.

It's like fishin' for dick!

She had Mark's in her hand now, realizing that the punter—the smallest of the three players—had the biggest equipment. She held on a little longer, gave him a squeeze, letting him know she'd chosen him. He let her hold him and winked at her with a very blue eye. The other two were circling again, and she didn't mind letting their hands caress her goosebumped skin. Kevin's fingers reached slyly between her rounded buttocks, right past the tiny slip of black cloth she still wore. Andy's thumb and forefinger circled and pinched one of her stiff nipples.

"Now now," she chided, "you guys are sure grabby!"

But she was still holding Mark's member, so she didn't shake them off. Besides, they were sure heating her up. She could feel the vibrations starting deep down in her secret places. She gazed into each set of eyes in turn and knew they all wanted her.

Was she ready to take all three?

When had she ever turned down a challenge?

They were standing in about five feet of water, on a sandy bottom. She felt an occasional fin brush past, but she knew there were fishies in the lake, nothing to worry about. No piranhas, no crocodiles, no anacondas—*well, at least none actually belonging to the snake family!* she chuckled—nothing out of some bad movie like those Mandi always made her watch on movie night. The guys clearly weren't worried about sea creatures either, other than the mermaid they had standing between them.

Kevin dunked his head down below the water's surface and next she felt his face nuzzling the globes of her ass.

"Mmmmm," she moaned. *That* was a particular turn-on.

Not to be outdone, Andy's lips snagged her rock-hard nipple. She tilted her head back, enjoying the multiple sensations. In her hand, Mark's dick swelled and she almost gasped.

This was getting too good for amateur hour.

Krystal wondered, were these guys ready to put their equipment to the test?

The last time she'd been in a threesome it hadn't gone well. She'd had a great time with Rachel, but Rachel's boyfriend Sam had felt left out even when they'd tried really hard. She still saw Rachel for a quickie now and again, but Rachel had moved on and Sam had found some religious nutcase to warm his bed, and she wondered what *that* was like, but no fuckin' thanks, not for her.

But now with three guys swirling all over her, she was ready to step it up a notch.

"Children," she said, her voice husky and suggestive, "I think we should move on up to land where we're not getting wedgies by the wildlife, okay?"

The three were reluctant to let her go without them, so all four edged toward the pier where there was a ladder they could climb. She'd noticed there was a diving raft anchored a ways out in the tiny bay, and that might have been fun in the hot sun, but it was getting on toward night. As if to remind them, the dock lights flicked on and bathed the water in a bright light. They climbed up the ladder one by one, her first, and she watched the guys' muscles and dicks when they followed eagerly.

"To the boathouse!" she said, figuring it might be open because of the party. They could claim it earlier than anyone else.

"Lead on, Krystal," said Mark, and his friends concurred.

A dozen yards away the squat structure thrust out over the rich man's fake harbor, and as they approached Krystal noted it was two stories, with a deck wrapped around the upper portion. The door was—*score!*—open, and inside they saw the empty slip where two boats could be housed, but more interestingly the stairs that led upstairs. Krystal giggled as she slapped football player butt and led the three on a merry chase up the steps. They climbed up through a square trapdoor and found themselves inside a well-appointed paneled den or living room set-up, with leather sofas and couches and armchairs facing the center, where some kind of black wood stove hunkered on the floor with a pipe reaching up and through the ceiling.

"Sweet!" Andy had found a light switch and now subtle sconces gave the place a romantic vibe.

"Sure, Jason's folks are loaded," Mark reminded Andy.

"This is a perfect fuck-den!" said Kevin, grabbing Krystal's hand and gently pulling her toward the nearest sofa.

Before she knew it, she was on the cool leather, her knees curled up under her, with the naked players lined up in front, playing a version of musical chairs with her mouth. She paid Mark's dick particular attention while using her hands to keep the other two interested. The boys groaned as she worked their flesh with fingers and lips and tongue, and Krystal enjoyed controlling them so easily. She was planning the next phase, which she hoped would include at least two of them attempting something she'd heard of but hadn't yet tried. She figured this was her chance, and she was taking it.

Meanwhile she'd struck the three dumb with amazement

as she used her finely-honed skills to bring them to the brink and back multiple times, giving each extra attention for a few minutes before switching.

They were intent on their own party so they barely heard the downstairs door open and close.

Someone had entered the boathouse, but the way things were going there was little chance the four adventurous teenagers were going to stop what they were doing. In fact, the heat they were generating had quickly dried their chilled wet skin.

A foot fell on the stairs and then another. And another, and another. The footfalls were slow, heavy, ponderous. One of the climbing feet seemed to be dragging.

"Oh, yeah, baby!"

"Come on, now, you're doin' it!"

"There, right there!"

"Mmmmmmm."

"Hey?"

"Don't worry," Krystal said, licking her lips. Her jaw was getting sore. "I've got other plans." She grabbed hold of Kevin and positioned him in front of her, then dragged Mark down onto the sofa and climbed over him. Andy got it right away, standing and waiting for the position to work itself out. Krystal reached down. "Mark, you're going where no one's ever been!"

There was a mumble of pleasant agreement, and then all hell broke loose.

Whoever had been climbing the steps reached the second level and stepped onto the floor.

Kevin called out, "Hey, who's there?"

"Jason, that you?" Andy said, squinting in the half-light.

All four heads turned as they paused the action.

It *was* Jason, but he was shambling closer slowly, almost dragging his feet. One foot. And there was somebody behind him.

98

"Crap! Man, Jason, sorry about this—"

"Oh God, yeah, Jason, we can get the hell out of—"

Krystal said, "Jason, where's Anna? You want in on this?"

But Jason wasn't saying anything. He approached and then they could see that behind him was Tyler. He was dragging, too. And they were bringing a smell closer. No, not a smell—a *stench*.

Krystal got a whiff and gagged. It was the first time since she'd jumped in the water.

"What the fuck—?"

"Look, man, we were just—"

Jason had reached them now, and suddenly he was standing in enough light for them to see...

Really see.

That he was just about naked, bruised, and that his groin area was bloody and mangled. Ruined. Almost as if...as if somebody had ripped him open where his junk used to be. And his head, it looked as if it had been crushed in a vise, the bones of his skull protruding.

But that wasn't even the worst.

No, because behind him they now saw Tyler, Mandi's lovely Tyler, hunched over with a hand reaching behind him, where he seemed to have dragged up a *tail*, or a rope, or...?

Impossibly, he had dragged a long section of his own intestines up the stairs behind him.

Krystal screamed, the aborted sexual escapade forgotten, and tried to leap off Mark's withered loins to race for the door or just *somewhere*, but faster than anyone could have expected Jason and Tyler—or whatever they had become— each snatched a couple limbs and pulled the four confused and horrified teens to the floor.

And fell upon them, ripping and tearing.

HALF
TIME

FIRST
ACT

"Damn it, turn off that light, Gordy."

"But I can't see a damn thing, Bud."

"Well, if you'd keep that motherfucking light off and let your eyes adjust you would be able to see just fine. We just gotta get through these woods. When we get to the lakeshore we should be able to find our way to the marsh. Then we'll be able to see a lot better."

"Well, why can't I use the light until we get to the shore?"

"Let's see…A, this is private property we're trespassing on. B, shining deer ain't exactly legal. And third, because I said so, dumb-ass. That's why. Now keep that light off and follow me."

"How am I supposed to follow you when I can't see?"

"If you'd shut your face and wait a minute your eyes would adjust to the dark."

"I don't like it, Bud. Why can't we just go huntin' somewheres else?"

"Because the deer are in the marsh, dumb-ass."

"There are probably deer in old man Guttmann's field, too. And it won't be so hard to get there."

"Are you listening to me, Gordy? Somebody will see us if we're in Theodore Guttmann's corn field. There's a clear view all the way to the road. And it ain't no sure thing like the marsh. There's always deer around that marsh, all year round."

"*Wait*. Wait, Bud. Did you hear that?"

"What?"

"Did you hear that noise?"

"No, I didn't hear a damned thing."

"Wait, there it is again. Sounds like somebody's following us."

"Don't you turn that damn light on, Gordy."

"Damnit Bud, I wanna see."

"Nobody is following us, Gordy. If you hear something it's some critter out there. Way more scared of us than we are of it. Now let's just slowly proceed towards the marsh. We ain't got all night."

"There it was again, Bud. Didn't you hear it? Right behind us."

"No Gordy, I didn't hear nothin'."

"But Bud, I...I...*Gaaaalck*...

"Gordy, goddamnit I told you to keep that damn light off. You got the damn thing shinin' right into my damn face, I can't see a fuckin' thing. Now pick it up and let's get going. Gordy? Gordy, you all right? Gordy is that you? Stop messin' around. Pick up that light and turn the damn thing off. Are you listenin' to me? Gordy? What the hell you doin'? Wait, Gordy, get that knife outta my face! Hey Gordy! *EEEEEIIIIIGGHH!!!!*"

SECOND ACT

She had been walking for an hour. Or was it longer? Maybe two hours?

Anna wasn't sure. She'd left her damn phone behind, maybe in the tent. *That was stupid.*

Although how much service would there have been around here, anyway, in the middle of fuck-all anywhere?

The woods were darkening fast. The light from above the treetops was fading, like it always does in late summer. It was probably going to get cold, too. Suddenly those stupid bonfires and passed around bottles of terrible tasting booze sounded pretty good. And maybe having sucked Jason's dick once would have been a small price to pay for the use of a real, luxurious bathroom whenever she wanted it.

It was just he was such a jerk about it, such an entitled rich-boy, suck my dick because I'm too great for you to pass up, A-1 entitled jerk asshole!

She stopped walking just to stamp her foot twice. It felt good.

Then she heard the rustle of something large moving around not too far away, behind a screen of tree trunks that stood like sentries in a line.

"J-Jason?" she whispered.

It had to be Jason, who followed her and was now going to play some game. Suck his dick? Hell, she'd cut it off when she finally saw him, smart-ass face standing there, looking at her with his superior genes and whatever else…

There it was again, the sound of someone walking

through thick undergrowth, but trying to be careful about it.

Someone?

Something?

"Come on out of there, Jason Carruthers, you asshole!"

At this point, she would have welcomed even his sarcastic frat-boy face. He *did* have a nice dick, she thought. *Damn my morals!* Maybe it wouldn't have been so—

Then a terrible, awful, disgusting stench hit her full in the face and she gagged.

What the hell?

Sounded like someone was about to crash through the bushes right in front of her.

Anna turned and ran as fast as she could in the opposite direction, skirting tree trunks and roots and thick bunches of weird-looking vegetation. She ran a zig-zag pattern that confused her sense of direction even more than it had been.

Suddenly it was completely dark. She stumbled to a stop, hearing no sound of pursuit.

But now she was even more lost than before.

Anna started crying.

THIRD
QUARTER

CHAPTER
THIRTEEN

Kaylee Williams' ears perked up. She listened past the singing crickets and mused to herself about whether or not the night's darkness enhanced her hearing. She turned her head, tuning in. There it was—an engine roaring in the distance. Kaylee guessed it was still about a half-mile away, but approaching fast. She could tell they were making the turn at the bottom of the hill, gunning it around the corner. She stopped walking, thrust out her thumb, and waited.

Before long a set of high beams crested the hill, first lighting the treetops then cutting lower and lower across the vegetation until Kaylee could clearly see the headlights brightening the two-lane blacktop highway...and bearing down on her fast.

She knew she was in trouble when she noticed the light-bar on the car's roof. The gold and black paint scheme and the word *Sheriff* splashed across the door drove the point home.

Shit.

The car slowed quickly and stopped with a gravelly crunch and Kaylee heard the electric whine of the car's passenger-side window descending. She leaned down and peered through the empty space at the car's occupant. By the glowing green and orange dashboard lights she could barely make out Deputy Harris at the wheel.

"Hey there, Kaylee," said the deputy. He was smirking.

"Doug," Kaylee replied, nodding.

"Um...please call me Deputy Harris while I'm on duty."

"Fine, Deputy Harris it is."

"So, where are you headed, babe?"

"Anywhere but here."

"Yeah. Well, you're gonna worry your grandma half to death. Then I'm gonna hear all about it. So why don't you just get in and I'll give you a ride back home."

The door unlocked with a loud click. He patted the seat.

Like I'm a dog and I'm gonna jump in.

"Why don't you give me a ride to the Greyhound station?"

"Come on, Kaylee...you know I cain't rightly do that... Hop in."

Kaylee said nothing. This was exactly what she'd hoped to avoid.

Doug was smiling at her with a crooked grin on his fuzzy, unshaven face. He was only a few years older but he always tried to act experienced. To think she'd had a crush on him when she was a kid! Lord knew, she couldn't figure out why now. Now he was just a hick town sheriff's deputy. And he thought she wanted him. She still refused to answer.

"You know I can arrest you for hitchhiking, right?"

"You wouldn't," she whispered hoarsely.

"I'd have to," he said slowly, like talking to a child. "I could get in trouble otherwise."

She didn't buy it, but she sighed. "Can I sit in back?"

"No, that's for prisoners and perps. You ride up here with me."

Kaylee opened the passenger side door and slid into the seat. It was over. She slid as close to the door as possible.

"Thanks," the deputy said. "I didn't want to have to arrest you. Your grandma would have killed me. Hey, is that a new tattoo?" he added, his eyes glinting.

Something to talk about, maybe. Something that would make her like him? Or maybe he just dug tattooed chicks?

Kaylee looked down at the colorful sleeves that covered

her bare arms. A kaleidoscope of roses, stars, butterflies, skulls, and pin-up girls tastefully laid out blended to give the effect of a grand design, all on full display outside the confines of the tight black halter top she wore. "Nope," she said. "All the same tats."

"Yeah, well...you got so many, it's hard to tell." Deputy Harris leered at her. Or was he just looking at her fondly? She couldn't tell. His tone was almost mocking. He made a Y-turn on the two-lane highway. "So, where exactly were you goin', anyway?"

"Nowhere. *Anywhere*. Jesus, Doug. I fit in here about as well as a racehorse in a pigpen. I don't want to be stuck here married to some fat greasy farmer five years from now with four kids and thighs like a hippopotamus. I want to go to the city. I want to find people with my same interests. I want to be somewhere where the only night life isn't drinking a six pack, getting laid in the back of Tommy Halstead's pickup truck, and listening to the damned farm report. Hog futures! Who cares? Where am I going? Nowhere, Doug. I'm going *nowhere*."

Her voice faded, the last word a desperate whisper. She slapped the dashboard lightly, wanting to punch it, but what was the point?

Her last attempt to leave had also been thwarted.

"Oh, come on Kaylee, it's not that bad here. I've been to the big city. It's full of hustlers, liars, and fast-talking con men. You're just young and full of piss and vinegar, that's all. In a few years this'll pass and you'll be glad you're right where you are."

Did he almost add: with me?

"I doubt that," Kaylee said, hanging her head and sighing. She couldn't believe he'd said *piss and vinegar*. Just proved she had good reason to want to bail. It's like he was living in a movie from the Fifties. They *all* were. Escape was the only way out, but she kept getting stopped.

Her grandma had a lot of pull. It was like that movie she saw, where the East Germans were trying to get over the wall, and they'd get shot and killed and then there'd be a cross painted on the wall to mark their death. What would mark her death, *her* foiled escape attempt?

"You just wait and see."

Doug Harris didn't understand *at all*.

And the last thing she wanted was to be with him. He struck her as a secret perv, not that she knew anything actual. But she'd heard rumors...

Static crackled over the radio, followed by the dispatcher's voice. *"Hey Doug, we've got a murder reported at the Carruthers place, 744 Lake Crest Drive."*

"Jesus!" Deputy Harris said with a gasp. "What?"

He punched his hand-held: "Hello, Rose, uh...can you please repeat? Sounded like you said *murder*."

"Ten-four, Doug. Called in that way, but...Sounds more like a bunch of college kids getting drunk and trying to pull a fast one. We just need you to check it out. Maybe somebody passed out and looks dead, I dunno."

"Damn city kids," the deputy said, aiming the sideways comment at Kaylee. Then into the radio: "All right, Rose, I'll check it out. Heading over there now. Over." He looked at Kaylee and winked. "You better fasten your seatbelt," he said, like it was a line from a movie. Then he mashed his foot down on the accelerator and they roared away.

CHAPTER FOURTEEN

It was the beating that drew his attention. The continuous drone of a rhythmic pulse that was almost overpowering. He could feel it vibrating through him as well as around him. He held his torch out ahead of himself, following the sound.

In the fluttering light cast from the torch's flame he could see the hearts—dozens of them, maybe even hundreds out beyond the torchlight—impaled on stakes thrusting up from the ground. And still beating. A fresh rivulet of blood coursing down the shaft of each stake with every pulse.

At the light's farthest reach, where the shadows were as thick as a starless sky just past midnight, he could make out a figure.

He approached warily, drawn in by the drumbeat of a thousand synchronized disembodied hearts.

The figure had its back to him, and it was wearing a long black hooded cloak. When he was almost near enough to touch it, she turned around.

A tiny clasp held the cloak around her neck. The hood shrouded the features of her face, but the cloak itself was open, exposing her naked body, young and perfect and... *bloody.* He could make out the multiple wounds on her chest and abdomen, crimson fluid bubbling from them in rhythm with the beating hearts. In her right hand she clutched a gleaming dagger.

Though he couldn't make out her face, he felt as if he knew this woman.

She stepped aside, allowing him to see the goat that stood behind her. The creature's massive horns curled up over its head. It stared up at him with its pupils just visible in their horizontal slits.

The heart drumbeat gradually increased its speed until the heartbeats were racing.

The woman turned, her cloak veiling the goat from sight as she lifted the dagger high over her head a thrust it down over and over, the goat bleating horribly as its blood spurted in high arcs that followed the dagger's blade.

He couldn't stand the sound. The animal's screams chilled his blood.

He pushed the woman aside and found that the cloak was empty black smoke which dissipated as his hand passed through it. His waving hand cut through the dark cloud, and he fought to see what lay beyond it. As the smoke dispersed he became aware that the goat was gone. In its place a young man was spread out face-up on the ground, the dagger still buried in his chest.

The man reached up for him.

"Uncle Tim...Uncle Tim."

Professor Tim Wallace sprang up into a seated position, disoriented, heart racing. He had drifted to sleep on the couch. He wiped the sweaty sheen from his brow, the ever-present ticking of clocks suddenly reminiscent of a bomb timer.

Danny was in trouble.

Professor Wallace cursed himself. He should have trusted his instincts. He shouldn't have let Danny go. Not there. Not back *there*.

He eyed the nearly empty Jack Daniels bottle and rocks glass on the coffee table in front of him. A half-inch of water that had recently been ice cubes was the only thing remaining in the glass, tempting him to refill it. *Just a quick nip.* He fought the urge. Danny's life might be at stake. Groggily he grabbed his keys and his phone. There was no time to waste. He headed out to his car parked in the driveway.

He had to get to Killdeer Lake. Maybe there was still time.

CHAPTER FIFTEEN

Deputy Doug Harris had his light bar flashing red and blue and pulsed his siren as he pulled up in front of the fancy lake house. College kids scattered out of the way, eyeing the deputy with fear and suspicion. Maybe with disdain, too, since they were all rich asshole kids. But apparently they didn't know what was going on, Kaylee thought, given their expressions.

Doug stopped the car, leaving the transmission in park. He grabbed a Maglite. "You stay here, Kaylee. I'm gonna see what's happening."

Kaylee gave him a slight acknowledging wave before he sighed and climbed out. Then Kaylee slid out the passenger door right behind him.

On hearing Kaylee's door slam shut, Doug turned. "I said stay in the car! Are you deaf?"

He tried to stare her down. Kaylee shrugged. It didn't work.

The deputy shook his head. He headed for the front door, which was splashed in the alternating blue and red strobe from his squad car. Kaylee followed, undaunted.

Though there were plenty of students scattered around—laughing and drinking on the lawn—a mass of them seemed to be concentrated on the front porch. A couple scurried down the stairs to meet Doug before he reached them, obviously relieved the cavalry had arrived. They seemed upset. Whatever was happening, their reactions seemed genuine enough, Kaylee thought.

"Officer, officer, this way!" a freaked-out, bare-chested young guy called out.

He looked like an athlete of some sort to Kaylee. Big, muscular. Maybe football?

"There's a killer out there!" the shirtless boy blurted out, barking out the syllables as if it were one long word and pointing out into the darkness as he did. "And our friend Mandi was almost killed!"

"Hold on, son," Deputy Doug said. "What are you saying?"

Kaylee thought it odd that Doug would refer to the guy as *son*. After all, these students looked like they were roughly the same age as the young deputy, maybe just a year or two younger.

"I'm serious, officer, and Mandi needs help!"

"Whoa, let's take this one thing at a time." Doug said. He was speaking calmly on purpose, Kaylee thought, to keep the kid from freaking even more. "Is she hurt, son?"

"I don't think so, it's hard to tell," the athletic kid said. "She's hysterical," he added as he led Doug back up onto the porch and pointed. Doug had the Maglite on now and he pointed it.

Kaylee lingered behind, standing at the foot of the steps. The harsh light beam revealed a girl curled up on herself, hugging her knees, wearing only an imprinted t-shirt, sitting on a white wicker love seat. She did seem to have blood on her skin, and some had soaked through the thin shirt. Nearby stood another sweaty hulking guy in a t-shirt. The scared kid with the hard-body had obviously donated the shirt.

Thumping hip-hop pulsed from inside, but the door must have been massive because it was barely audible out here. Lights blinked on and off, and shadows in the nearby windows indicated the party was in full swing. It wasn't out of control, not yet.

"Young lady," Doug said after taking a long look. "Can you tell me what happened?"

The girl just stared, her eyes as wide as headlights. Her head moved in small, jerky motions, like a twitch.

The bare-chested kid went off when he saw that Doug was only interested in Mandi. "Officer, what about the killer?"

Doug lowered the beam. "Calm down, son."

There he goes with the "son" again!

"Calm down my ass! That...that *thing*, whoever or whatever, it killed two of my friends! Right in front of me! I watched it happen! And Mandi was running away from it. She was naked, so I gave her my shirt." He was starting to babble.

The girl—*Mandi? like in the song*, Kaylee thought illogically—was still unresponsive, her eyes like blank mirrors, so Doug faced the distraught guy. The kid was almost jumping out of his skin.

"Why don't you tell me what happened, son?"

Argh, Kaylee thought. *Face-palm.*

Kaylee climbed the few steps softly and sidled up behind the kid and the cop. Nobody noticed.

"Well, we were..."

"Start with your name, please."

"Rob Klein."

"Age?"

"Twenty-one."

"You been drinking tonight, Robert? Got an ID?"

"I had a couple beers." The kid fumbled a card from his pocket and Doug shined the Maglite on it.

"Do you use drugs?"

"No." The boy hesitated before answering. Kaylee thought he was lying. But she rolled her eyes. Doug was ignoring Mandi, who looked like she'd been scared to death. *Literally.*

"You from around here, Robert?" He handed back the ID.

"No. I'm at the university."

"Okay, I knew that from your ID. Why don't you tell me what happened?"

"Me and my friends were out by the fire pit waiting for everybody to show up. Then Mandi jumped out of the woods naked and bloody and screaming that someone killed Tyler, and…"

"This is Mandi?" Doug interrupted, pointing at the girl in the t-shirt. She didn't look up.

Well, duh, Deputy Doug, Sherlock of the backwoods. Kaylee rolled her eyes.

"Yes."

"And who is Tyler?"

"Tyler's her boyfriend. I told you."

"Okay, go on."

"We tried to retrace her steps—where she came from in the woods—to see what she was running away from, and we ran into this…this *guy*, with an axe and he killed Marlon and Doug with it. Oh my God, he chopped'em right in the head…" The boy trailed off. He seemed suddenly lost in his own mind.

"Can you describe your assailant?"

Rob came back from wherever he'd been. "No, he had some kind of costume on. Like a skeleton or something."

"So you're telling me that a guy dressed as a skeleton with an axe killed both your friends in the woods and none of you tried to disarm him? You let him get away?"

"Yes…yeah, we wanted to but he was quick. I'm tellin' you, he was *fast*. It all happened so fu—uh, fast…so unexpected."

Deputy Doug turned to the other musclebound guy. "How about you, you see any of this?"

The kid shook his head. "Nah, I was here havin' a beer. I'm twenty-two. But I seen Mandi naked and all covered in blood…"

Just then the front door opened, letting out more and louder music, and a man walked out. An older man, he seemed refined and gave off an aura of power. In his left hand he held a scotch glass the bottom quarter of which contained a brown liquor. Kaylee squinted to see him better. He had a full head of salt and pepper hair, a little gray soul patch on his chin, dark piercing eyes, and he was dressed casually but in a way that implied wealth. He didn't look like he belonged there, with all the dumb college jocks and their chicks.

"What's going on here?" asked the older guy.

"Mr. Carruthers," Doug said, stepping back. He looked awestruck.

"Doug," he nodded politely, glancing at the lit-up squad car. "What's happened?"

Jesus, this rich guy knows Doug?

"Looks like the kids here are just getting a little out of hand," Doug said with some authority, swinging his hand up to rest on his belt.

"Out of hand!" The Robert kid yelled. "There's a killer out there and you say we're getting out of hand! Didn't you hear anything I said?"

Doug waved his hand as if sweeping Robert's words aside for the moment.

"Wait, what's all this about a killer?" Mr. Carruthers asked, his head tilting.

"I think they just had a fast one pulled on them, sir. Nothing to be concerned about," Doug said, completely downplaying everything he'd heard and seen. "Too much beer, and maybe some illicit substances."

Kaylee couldn't believe it. *Sherlock? No way. Deputy Doofus, more like.*

It was great. Kaylee realized no one was aware of her. She melted into the shadows on the porch, edging closer to the still immobile Mandi, and just listened. She reached out a small hand and put it on Mandi's shoulder. The girl was shivering from the inside, and it freaked her. She dropped the hand.

"I want to hear more," Mr. Carruthers insisted, taking a step toward Doug, who deflated a little.

The boy—Robert, Rob—related a variation of his story a second time. It seemed to Kaylee that Mr. Carruthers was watching the girl (*Mandi?*) out of the corner of his eye the whole time. Looking right *through* Kaylee.

"I think you should call your dad, Doug," Mr. Carruthers said after Rob was finished in a breathless rush.

"But, sir," Doug pleaded. "I think I can handle…"

"Doug," said Mr. Carruthers, with unbending authority in his tone. "I want your dad on this one."

The deputy sighed like a chided five year old, turned, and tromped down the stairs past Kaylee back to his car. Kaylee listened in as he made the call on his radio. "Yeah, Rose… Can you get the sheriff out here?" Then a pause, followed by: "Yes I know he's home, Rose. But Mr. Carruthers requested his presence." second short pause, and then: "Nah, not sure about a murder. But something's going on." Pause. "Okay, thanks Rose."

Doug stood clear of the car and stiffly announced, "Sheriff's on his way, sir."

Doofus Doug, Kaylee thought.

CHAPTER SIXTEEN

Mr. Carruthers turned to Rob. "Why don't you help your friend into the house?" He made a small nod, referring to Mandi. "She looks like she's been through hell."

For the briefest of moments Carruthers noted a flash of disgust cross Rob's face, as if to say *No shit!* But the young man didn't say it, instead meekly following the elder Carruthers' suggestion, helping Mandi to her feet and leading her into the house while Jason's dad held the door open for them with his free hand.

"Everybody in the house!" They could hear Deputy Harris yelling from outside on the lawn. "I'm going to need everyone in the house right now!"

Rob helped Mandi to one of the plush leather couches, one of several facing the enormous fireplace, and let her collapse on it. He didn't seem to care about the blood stains.

Then Rob turned to Carruthers. "We need to get some guns and go hunt that thing down!" The tremble was audible in his voice.

"Let's let the sheriff and his deputy handle this, son. Having a bunch of frightened kids out there with loaded guns is the last thing we need."

"But you didn't see that...*thing!*"

"Look...Rob is it? My son is still out there somewhere, and I don't want some high-strung, terrified, half-drunk kid out there shooting at him. Understand? Now, let me get something to help your friend."

"But Jason—" Rob began.

"Yes, what about Jason?"

Rob looked down. "Never mind."

Carruthers climbed the main staircase to the upper floor, draining the remaining Scotch as he went and placing the empty glass on a nearby shelf as he passed. He made his way down one of the long corridors in the east wing to his massive personal bathroom. There, he opened the medicine cabinet and rifled through the assortment of medications until he found what he was looking for, a powerful prescription sedative. The same one he often slipped his wife when she was overreacting. He dumped one of the capsules into his hand and filled one of the glasses that rested near the sink with water. This would help the girl. *Perfect.*

He descended a second set of stairs nearer the back of the house, emerging just outside of his library which he had designated *off-limits*. He stepped inside for a moment to appraise his gun cabinets, thinking of what the kid Rob had said. The guns were for sport. He didn't need guns for safety. The world needed protection from *him*.

Smiling mirthlessly he returned to the great room and handed Mandy the capsule and glass of water. "Here you are, child. This should relax you and make this ordeal easier to handle."

"What are you giving her?" Rob said, his tone accusatory.

Carruthers held his temper. "It's a mild sedative. It will help to calm her nerves. Would you like one?"

"No thanks."

Mandi silently downed the pill and curled up in a ball on the couch.

"Someone should help clean you up, dear." Mr. Carruthers said to Mandi. He spied the girl from the porch nearby. "You, yes you, what's your name?"

"Me? Kaylee."

"Kaylee, why don't you take her to the main guest bathroom and clean her up? I'll show you the way."

"Shouldn't the police record her condition first?"

Carruthers bit his tongue. The child was a pain. "I'm sure in this case it's all right, it's not her blood. And it's getting on my furniture."

Kaylee shrugged.

Then he and Kaylee helped Mandi to her feet and led her to the one of the guest bathrooms where he left them to clean Mandi's skin of the caked-on blood. From there Carruthers made his way to his ground level bar, filled a second glass, and wandered back to await the sheriff's arrival.

Carruthers stood on his porch, sipped his expensive scotch, looking out past the flashing red and blues of the Deputy's car. The dark had settled in on the lawn and woods behind it. The sky was spattered with stars. Insect songs filled the air.

Most of the kids seemed to have moved inside where the deputy was taking their statements, though he was mostly just keeping them corralled. A few had escaped the deputy's scrutiny remaining outdoors and they stood in clusters, speaking in whispers broken by loud nervous laughter and morbidly humorous remarks. Carruthers was more interested in what the insects had to say.

He was calm, almost unnaturally so. It was a product of power. Sebastian Carruthers was in command of his world. He had mastered life physically, intellectually, and spiritually. Not much could shake his steely edifice.

The gravel crunched under a set of tires. The sheriff eased his car nose to tail with his son's squad. Carruthers strolled down the steps to greet the sheriff.

"Good evening, John." Carruthers said as the portly, balding sheriff climbed out of the gold and black cruiser.

Sheriff Harris grunted in response before dropping his ranger-style hat with the county sheriff's emblem on its crown above a pair of wind strings over his mostly bald head. He stepped clear and tried to hike up his duty belt and holster over his beer belly before asking, "What's going on, Sebastian?"

"Interesting things, John. I thought maybe you'd need to investigate."

"Couldn't we have let the boy make that call?"

Carruthers shrugged. "The boy doesn't have a whole lot of experience."

They walked side-by-side and made their way back to the house. "What exactly is the situation?"

"Looks like we may have a murderer on the loose."

The sheriff stopped in his tracks. "You gotta be shitting me."

"No, John. That's what they're saying inside, anyway. Sounds like at least three victims. Maybe. Nobody's seen them recently."

"You don't seem too upset by that."

"They're city kids, most of'em. They've come up here to the wilderness and gotten high on booze and lord knows what else. They hear a noise in the woods and run screaming. Somebody's probably standing out there watching, laughing their asses off. Of course, now that you're here they're probably afraid to come near the house. But that's not what I wanted to talk to you about."

"What's that?"

"We'll get to it, in time."

"So you think this whole thing is a prank?"

Carruthers shrugged. Where was Jason? Was he behind this? If he found out that was the case, he'd have a few choice words for his son. And indeed he might well consider sending Jason out of state to finish his degree—that would be an appropriate lesson.

As they mounted the steps, a pair of whispering kids on the porch went dead silent and waited for them to pass. The two men entered the house and found Deputy Doug and a large group of the remaining college students in the living room. Doug was standing with a notepad in hand, and most of the kids were seated on the various couches and chairs, except for some who were sitting on the floor.

When the sheriff entered, his deputy—who was also his son—came over to brief his superior.

"What have you got here, Doug?" the sheriff asked quietly.

"Kind of a mess."

While the deputy talked with the sheriff and brought him up to speed on the stories being told, Sebastian Carruthers's eyes roamed the room while his mind roamed the ether, drifting.

Nearby, the local law stopped their whispering.

"Well," the sheriff sighed. "Shall we go and find our culprits?"

Doug nodded, his eyes full of excited anticipation.

The sheriff shot him down. "Not you. You stay here and watch over the house. Keep all these people inside. Take more notes. If anything happens, radio me." Then, addressing Carruthers, he gestured with a shoulder and said, "Let's go."

"So you think it's a prank?" Sheriff Harris asked Carruthers when they were outside and alone.

Mr. Carruthers shrugged. "We're the most dangerous things out here, John."

"Where's Jason?" the sheriff asked. "I didn't see him, and Doug says he didn't either."

"I don't know, but his girlfriend's here somewhere…"

"Could they be behind this?"

"If that's the case, John, he's definitely more than grounded." He chuckled. "Who're the supposed victims?"

"The girl's boyfriend, a biker-type name of Tyler…"

"Don't know him," Carruthers interrupted.

"And I guess two others who haven't been seen except by the Klein kid. Names are Marlon Jeffries and Greg, uh, Greg Watts. They're talking an axe murderer in there, Sebastian."

"Not very likely, is it? I think either a prank or some sexual shenanigans, or hurt feelings...or all three."

"From what I could see, the blood on the girl looked real enough." The sheriff turned to Carruthers with a hard glare. "By the way, what's with the sedative? You don't have the legal right—"

"My house, John. My kid's friends. My kid's party." He glared back. "I have every right, don't I?"

The sheriff sighed. "Okay for now. But if this gets out of hand..."

"It won't," Carruthers said confidently. But he was starting to worry.

Where was Jason?

The pair made their way to the sheriff's squad car, where the sheriff reached inside and produced his own Maglite—a flashlight that was not only bright, but big enough to double as a club. Then they headed across the lawn and followed a rough path through the dark woods to where the fire pit was located—where the boy, Robert Klein, claimed two of his friends had died at the hands of a costumed axe-wielding lunatic. The light helped but it revealed nothing unusual. It was a long walk and they were winded when they arrived.

"Not as young as I used to be," the sheriff said, huffing.

"Nor I," Carruthers agreed, though he was nowhere near as winded.

They entered the clearing. The bonfire, left on its own, had diminished to a deep red glow. What had once been logs was now ash and ember, smouldering amid a ring of large field stones. Near the pit was the beer keg, and a pile of firewood that was scattered chaotically, which tended to corroborate the story Robert Klein told.

Spotting the stack of plastic cups, Sheriff Harris wasted no time tucking the flashlight under his arm and tapping himself a beer. He took a sip, leaving a mustache of foam on his upper lip. "Wouldn't want it to go to waste." He brought the light's beam back to bear on the scene.

"Bring the light back here," Carruthers said.

Sheriff Harris illuminated the ground near the scattered firewood while Carruthers knelt down to get a better look. The grass was wet. Carruthers ran his finger along one of the blades then examined his finger tip, stained crimson. The liquid was tacky, coagulating, not quite dry but close.

"Blood," Carruthers said, as if it weren't obvious.

Sheriff Harris nodded. He swallowed his mouthful of beer soberly. Then he used his flashlight to follow the crimson trail back into the woods. The sheriff gulped, then covered it up with a belch. "Should we follow it?"

"Through that? No, it'll be almost impossible in the dark, even with your flashlight. The girl said she first saw it near the tool shed. Let's look there."

The sheriff refilled his cup before the men left the clearing. Carruthers noticed the cop's hand was shaking. They followed the tree line at the edge of the lawn until they reached the gravel trail through the woods and to the lake.

Sheriff Harris shone the light on the trail, looking for any evidence of hooliganism. The unidirectional light source was almost useless for spotting anything in the woods, which became a wall of shadow under the flashlight's glow.

Sebastian Carruthers walked in silence while the sheriff drank his beer. Carruthers wasn't a particularly talkative man, always having preferred his own thoughts to company. His thoughts went to Jason, and whether he was caught in the throes of a prank that had gone bad.

They reached the spot where the trail broke off and sloped down to the lake. Harris turned his beam on the water, spotlighting the speedboat as it bobbed calmly on the lake's surface. Further down was the pontoon boat. He swept the beam sideways and over the large boathouse. All was quiet. But there was a light on in the second floor of the boathouse. He was about to mention it, but...

The sound of a snapping branch in the woods nearby made the sheriff swing the light onto the trees. The light reflected off the trunks and thick undergrowth, bathing everything beyond that in impenetrable shadow.

Carruthers felt unnerved, which was inconceivable to him. Nothing ever got to Carruthers. In this world, he was the master. Yet, for some reason he felt almost...*afraid*. It had always been a point of pride that he was tuned to his surroundings, intuitively reading every situation. It had been one of the *gifts*. It had been one of the benefits of all the sacrifices he had made.

And now he felt as if he were being observed, *stalked*. But the flashlight's beam revealed nothing.

Harris refocused the light on the boat and pier. All seemed normal. Then he checked the boathouse again, and the light was off. Had it been on at all, or was it just a reflection?

"Where is this tool shed?" the sheriff asked.

"Just up ahead," Carruthers said, still distracted by his sensation of being watched. "Follow the trail."

They made their way up the small rise to the shed, which suddenly seemed to be right in front of them. The sheriff kept his light trained on the open door while they approached it. The beam partly illuminated the shadows, and the slick lake of blood on the shed's floor was unmistakable. That, and the fact that the building had been ransacked—tools were obviously missing from their designated places on the pegboard and shelves, but many were scattered across the floor and workbenches.

The men remained just outside the shed's door looking in at the devastation. "You still think this might be a prank?" Sheriff Harris asked.

Carruthers shook his head, confused. His mind raced

for answers as the vague sense of danger congealed into something more substantial.

The flashlight beam gave the interior of the shed a harsh tint. The blood was the color of black paint, but the splatters were self-evident.

"Don't look much like a robbery, does it?" the sheriff mused. "I mean, first off, what's to rob in a shed? And it looks a helluva lot like somebody was killed here."

"Hmn." Carruthers was deep in thought.

"But why?"

"I think we should go to the Burial Ground."

"What?" The sheriff stared at him.

Sebastian Carruthers did not repeat himself.

Instead, he snatched the Maglite from the sheriff's hand and led the way further up the gravel path. They followed the trail until the gravel below their feet thinned and eventually changed over to hard-packed clay and dirt, and the path seemed to slowly fade into woods. Before long they left behind all trace of the trail and were pushing through the tangle of underbrush in the forest.

"What the hell! Why—?" The sheriff angrily protested.

Carruthers shushed him before stopping to listen.

"Why are we…"

"Shut up, John!"

Carruthers tilted his head, trying to listen, concentrating on their surroundings. Though he couldn't hear anything he was still dogged by the sense of being surveilled. Of being watched, or stalked. Had they been followed? Shadowed in the woods?

When he had convinced himself there was no immediate threat, he turned and they continued on, tripping on the undergrowth that grasped at their feet.

They came to the clearing.

With one sweep of their light, Carruthers knew that the site had been disturbed. A wide jagged hole had been opened in the soil. Grass and underbrush had been piled haphazardly all around it and the rest of the clearing was marked with violent clefts and divots. The implications were multiple, and staggering.

"Jesus!" Sheriff Harris said, pulling off his hat with one hand and nervously swiping the sweat from his head.

"Don't you dare speak that name here!" Carruthers barked angrily.

"Sorry," the sheriff said, cowering. "Looks like somebody dug her up."

"No. Looks like she *clawed* her way out."

The sheriff backed away a step, his eyes roving around them.

"But why? Why and *how*? What have we done?"

"*We* didn't do anything. That's what I wanted to tell you, the Lamb has returned."

"What are you talking about?"

"Wallace," Carruthers sighed. He hated having wasted all this time. "Her child. Our sacrifice. He's here, now. Back at the house."

"How do know that?"

"I saw him, John. He looks just like her."

"Maybe you're mistaken."

"I'm not mistaken! It was him. I know my own goddamn child for fuck's sake! Asmodeus has come to claim what he was promised. It's the only explanation."

"Well, what should we do, Sebastian?"

"I've been trying to think about it. We should recreate the ritual. Give him what we promised. We will present him in offering and renew our vows. We'll go back to the house. You leave and assemble the coven while I tend to the Lamb and the altar."

"I may not be able to get everyone together at this late hour, Sebastian."

"That's okay, get as many as you can. Come through

one of the secret passages. We don't want to upset the party guests."

"And what about all this? The murders? Is it all true?"

"If I had to guess, I would say so…"

Sebastian Carruthers wondered if he had doomed his own son.

FOURTH
QUARTER

CHAPTER
SEVENTEEN

Mandi was reclining in the enormous whirlpool tub. Kaylee had helped her strip out of the loaner shirt from that muscular football player type, and coerced her into the tub after turning on the water, then having tested the temperature of the water with her hand. Not too hot, not too cold, just right.

The poor traumatized girl seemed to be in a stupor. Kaylee wasn't sure if it was in response to the ordeal Mandi had endured or if the sedative that the rich old guy—what was his name... Carruthers?—had slipped her.

Taking a plush washcloth from a nearby towel rack, Kaylee dipped it into the warm water that was slowly but persistently rising. Now about an inch of water pooled in the basin. Once wet, she gently slid the washcloth gently over Mandi's breasts, stomach, and thighs, caressing rather than scrubbing.

The dried blood was stubborn. She pumped a modest amount of antibacterial soap from a bottle perched on the tub's edge onto the cloth, folding it and rubbing it together until it was covered in foamy lather. Then she repeated the task at hand, slipping the soap-slick cloth over Mandi's soft skin, leaving a gleaming trail of suds clinging to Mandi's breasts and abdomen, over her shoulders and down her legs, which were bent at the knee.

"Thank you," the girl said, gazing at Kaylee dreamily. Mandi reached up and tenderly touched Kaylee's hand, holding it and the cloth in place for a moment.

Is she...? Kaylee couldn't imagine it was anything but

135

the drugs that were making Mandi so responsive to her touch.

"You're welcome. Just relax while I clean you up."

Mandi's lids fluttered and she seemed to fall away in a haze again.

Kaylee looked at Mandi and wondered at how her night had changed. Running away, getting caught by Deputy Doug, and getting drawn into this...this *drama*. Definitely not how her day had started, with the frustration and usual depression. With the urge to *escape*.

Escape.

To see someone having actually escaped *something* terrible, whatever it was, had sobered her. This could be *her*, Kaylee Williams, covered in blood, traumatized, sedated, yielding to a stranger's intimate touch.

And it *was* intimate, wasn't it?

I mean, what am *I doing here?*

It was almost as if there was an aura of sensuality in and around the house. She'd sensed it when they had pulled up, but it hadn't registered until now, now that she had a naked woman lying in warm water in front of her. Her imagination offered up a series of images of what the college guys and women would have gotten up to later, if nothing strange had happened. Seemed like some had already started, from the sounds she remembered hearing coming from a few of the tents in the scattered tent city that had sprung up on the expansive lawn. That rich guy, Carruthers, he was a weird one, and maybe it was *his* influence over everything that she'd noticed. She just hadn't analyzed it until now. She remembered how he'd gazed at Mandi even while she seemed to be out of it, frightened half to death, and possibly worse.

Under her hands, Mandi's nipples had swollen to thick, hard nubs.

The blood reluctantly yielded to the warm, soapy

washcloth as Kaylee worked it in slowly measured movements over Mandi's youthful physique, rewetting it often in the filling tub. The process was cathartic, and Kaylee felt almost as if she were a part of Mandi's sedated dream. She eyed the coed's body and how it was reacting to her touch. Kaylee smiled as she continued bathing the woman who'd been placed in her care in this stranger's house full of strange and bizarre people.

In a weird way, Kaylee realized she was *enjoying* this whole experience.

Which was why the blood-curdling screams that suddenly came from the other side of the bathroom door were so shocking, immediately dropping Kaylee from a bizarre sort of heaven into a wide-open nightmare.

Her head snapped around to stare at the door she had instinctively locked, half expecting it to crash in on them.

There was more screaming, apparently both men and women, reacting in utter terror.

But reacting to *what*?

Kaylee couldn't exactly leave Mandi alone in the tub, not in her present condition. She might slide under and drown, even though the water was only about eighteen inches deep. Kaylee reached over and twisted the faucet until the warm cascade ended in a trickle.

"What's going on?" Mandi said, her voice drowsy. Her eyes were widening, but still under the sedative's thrall.

"I'm not sure," said Kaylee, eyeing the door warily. "Let's get you out of the tub and I'll go see."

"Why am I naked?"

"Uh, it's complicated."

Beyond the bathroom door something crashed loudly, followed by more screams.

"What's that? What's going on?"

Kaylee didn't know, but it didn't sound good. Not at all.

Keeping her cool, Kaylee helped the still-woozy Mandi

out of the tub, wrapping her in a towel. "Here, sit on the edge of the tub. I'll be right back," Kaylee told her charge.

" 'kay." Mandi sighed, her eyes starting to close again.

Kaylee unlocked the bathroom door. *Really, what's the worst thing that can be out there?* She wondered. A bunch of drunk frat boys getting into a fight? Wild drinking contests? But what if Mandi and that other guy—Rob?—were right and there actually *was* a costumed killer out there... somewhere? What if he *was* killing people? And what if he was in the house?

She shook her head. How likely was that? Deputy Doug was still around, right?

She went to the door and turned to assure Mandi, "Be right back." Then she slipped out and closed the door behind her.

In the long hall outside she heard a commotion that seemed to be coming from... *everywhere.* A metallic clanging rang out up ahead on her left, from what she assumed was the kitchen, where frantic and ominous shadows splashed chaotically against the tile floor. Beyond that, from the enormous living room, she could hear someone shouting, "Get back! Get back!"

Someone screamed in pure terror. The scream was cut off in a wet gurgle.

She needed to find that Rob kid. He'd seemed plenty brave. After all, he'd actually faced off against the murderer, hadn't he? *I mean, if there was a murderer.* He'd saved Mandi, right? Last time she had seen him, he was up ahead in that massive living room when she'd left to help Mandi clean up. That's where she'd start.

She jogged down the hall and rushed past the kitchen, trying to get a sense of the mayhem within without slowing down much. Better to keep moving! Even from a glance she could see a pair of muscular guys fighting. One of them was completely naked! Naked and blood-streaked. The other one looked like he was just about to set into the naked guy with a butcher knife!

God, what's happening?

Scurrying down the rest of the hall and away from the kitchen, Kaylee next dashed to the great room. She stopped short where the corridor opened into the living room, and some kind of expensive-looking crystal decoration smashed against the wall in front of her, missing her by inches. Glass shards flew in all directions and she barely felt some open up tiny wounds in her cheeks and forehead, missing her eyes miraculously.

Here she had no choice but to stop and survey the area.

Inside the room a horror show was playing out before her eyes. She blinked fast, checking to make sure her eyes were still working.

Most of the college kids had banded together in groups——a large bunch in one corner while other groups were made up of smaller numbers. They seemed to fighting off other kids, many of whom were buck naked. But there was something wrong with them. Terribly, ridiculously wrong. And the longer she looked on the more fucked up they appeared to be.

One of the boys—of the few who actually had clothes on—looked as if he'd been in a car accident. His head was half-crushed, and bone, blood, and brain matter was leaking out of what was left of his skull in a kind of pink stream. His jeans were ripped open at the crotch, a crimson gouge where his package had once been as if someone had taken a huge ice cream scoop to him.

Another one seemed to be trailing a length of his own intestines, which were hanging out of his ruined asshole. Drying bloodstains were on everyone she saw.

The only female *thing* that Kaylee could see sported a cute blonde pixie cut, and she was missing her lower jaw. It wasn't actually missing, it was just no longer attached to her face and instead she was brandishing it as a weapon.

What the fuck! (Even her religious mother would have allowed her to say the words this one time.)

These people weren't *people* anymore. They were like zombies from a bad horror movie (or novel, she'd read some of those).

These freakshows moved in jerky motions, like real-life Ray Harryhausen Dynamation monsters. But they were surprisingly fast. And dangerous. Deadly, in fact.

She shook her head, a strong sense of denial trying to keep her sanity in place.

Kaylee's brain struggled to accept what she was seeing. It just couldn't be real, could it? Was this all some sort of prank? A movie set she had wandered onto by mistake?

Kaylee watched, shocked, as the zombies or monsters or whatever the fuck they were pulled a screaming girl from one of the groups of rich jocks. Two of the creatures claimed her, playing tug-of-war with the screeching girl until—with supernatural strength—they ripped her still- howling head from her neck. The jawless girl then threw the head like a softball back at the group of teen and twenty-somethings, one of whom batted it away with what might have been a chair or table leg. The severed head bounced across the room, landing at Kaylee's feet. She started to scream, but it wouldn't come as she'd forgotten to suck in a breath while the crazed massacre unfolded in front of her.

To make matters worse, when the monsters dropped the headless coed to retrieve another victim, the headless corpse *rose up to help them!*

The screaming intensified as the number of normal college kids decreased, while the zombie population increased.

This was just too much.

Unable to watch any more, her stomach threatening to disgorge its contents, she started to retreat back down the hall but in that moment Kaylee couldn't help but look down at her feet. The dead girl's head stared back up at Kaylee with blind empty eyes, but its mouth opened and shut like a fish on a pier trying to gulp a watery breath.

Now an ear-piercing shriek broke loose from Kaylee's lips. Like a delayed effect reflex, she punted away the grotesque head into the center of the melee in the great room. She didn't stick around to see where it went.

CHAPTER EIGHTEEN

Kaylee turned to sprint back to the bathroom, thinking she could get Mandi out of there through the kitchen, but now the way was blocked by three party-goers—two males and a woman. And they were *not* having a good time.

Blood-stained and disfigured, none of them was remotely human any more. Their mouths were distended and their teeth clacked like castanets as they looked for something to crunch—and that something was Kaylee...

They advanced on her rather rapidly and had passed the bathroom door so she would have to fight through them to get to Mandi, if she was even still alive.

Kaylee feinted left and two of the animated corpses went for the trick, but the third did not and suddenly Kaylee felt an iron grip around her forearm. One of the football players had wrapped his huge sausage fingers around her and was squeezing so hard she felt the pain all the way to the bone.

And he was pulling her at the same time, pulling her toward his clattering mouth.

She squealed and tried backing out of his grip, but she couldn't. She tried suddenly relaxing her own pull to take him off-balance, but in the meantime the other two things were now grasping her hair and her other hand.

"Mandi, help me!" she managed to shout, hoping the dazed girl would wake up and somehow find a way to do something. Otherwise she was dead...

Before she could realize exactly what was happening, the thing who had grabbed her first made a gurgle with that horrific mouth of his and she couldn't believe it when a pointed metal tip punched out between his lips. Blood and teeth exploded out and sprayed across her face, but before she turned away she saw the college kid's eyes cross and then splatter across his cheeks like rotten grapes.

It was Rob, wearing a borrowed t-shirt and wielding a long fireplace poker like some kind of sword. After he yanked it out of Dead Guy One, he used it as a club across the head of Dead Girl, bashing in what was left of her skull. Brass and iron made a wet *squash* sound, like fruit getting blasted at a Gallagher concert. Kaylee couldn't believe she'd thought of that...how many kids her age even knew about the comic? Well, her parents were weird and watched that crap on TV when all she wanted to do was escape to elsewhere. In any case, the rod took care of the girl-thing's engine or whatever and it collapsed like a sack of bleeding guts.

"Where's Mandi?" Rob shouted. He was fending off Dead Guy Two with the poker, but this thing seemed to have learned how to avoid heavy pointy objects, because it kept dancing out of the way. "We've gotta get out of here!"

"Is it better out there?" she asked.

"Don't know, but it's like they're all in here, and out there we have cars. Any better ideas?"

"No. Mandi's in the bathroom, in the whirlpool. Naked."

"Damn this thing. He used to be a friend of mine, but he doesn't even know who I am now."

"You're food, I think."

"You think it's a zombie thing, like in the movies?" Rob asked, as he tried slashing his former friend with the poker.

"Who cares? All I know is they die, then they kill you, then you're like them. We can argue semantics later."

"Fuck yeah." Rob had had it. Former friend or not, he brained Dead Guy Two with the poker, creasing the guy's skull. Then, before the thing had a chance to register what had happened, Rob pulled the poker back and brought it down again hard with a wet *thwack* that rattled their teeth. The third time was the charm, and the thing dropped. Maybe dead, maybe not. They stepped over him and the path to the bathroom door was clear of zombies or whatever they were.

Kaylee was glad she didn't know any of these people. *Former* people. Might have made it harder to kill them. She thought they were probably more true to themselves now than they'd ever been while doing whatever jocks and hot sorority chicks and their friends do while wasting time and taking up space and oxygen in college.

But she was like that. Her parents had given up on her, and she had given up on them. This was why she'd been on her way out of this *hellhole* of a backwoods burg.

Tell me I'm not a fucking prophet, Kaylee thought. *If ever there was a perfect word for this place than "hellhole" I sure can't think of one...*

"Let's get Mandi and get the hell out," was what she said.

And as soon as she said it a couple more dead college kids roared down the hall right at them, coming from the kitchen...maybe the back door?

It didn't matter, both Kaylee and Rob had to fight their way through them to get to the bathroom. Assuming Mandi hadn't already been pulled out. If she had, then they'd be fighting her soon, too.

Rob slashed and thrust at the first kid.

"Tony! We were friends through high school, man!" Rob put the poker across the kid's head like a baseball bat. Chunks of flesh and bone flew off.

Tony responded with a snarl and went for Rob's throat, his teeth grinding and clacking like joke dentures, but the blood and skin Kaylee could see in his mouth wasn't a joke.

The kid was *big* and he was driving Rob back.

Kaylee grabbed a heavy vase that she could barely

lift from one of the art sconces spread down the hallway, and smacked the kid in the head. The vase broke, and Rob managed to thrust the poker through the kid-thing's right eye. Then, while Tony writhed on the end of the poker like an olive skewered by a toothpick, Kaylee had to turn and face the other menacing thing. This one was a girl not much older than she was who had been wearing a bursting-at-the-seams bikini at some point that day, but was now draped in mere wisps of cloth.

She must have been pret-ty popular, Kaylee thought just before the thing reached her. She was ready with a second vase. They lunged at each other, feinted, and she realized they'd been driven back from the end of the hall and the bathroom door...

And now there was that creepy old guy, what was his name? Carruthers, that was it. He'd been eyeing up Mandi like a pork chop, and sure enough there he was now, bursting into the bathroom and hustling poor Mandi out, still just wrapped in that big plush towel.

And there was Doofus Doug, helping him!

"Damn it, they're taking Mandi!" she shouted. She smashed the vase on the chick's head but missed and hit her more on the neck and shoulder. The girl-thing's crazy eyes locked on her and her claw-like hands reached for Kaylee's neck.

"Need a little help here!"

Somehow Rob materialized right beside her and swung the poker like a cross between a baseball bat and a golf club. The girl's eyes burst out of their sockets in bloody eruptions and Rob's poker bent as it smashed into the side of her head. He pulled it back and skewered her with it, driving her into the floor. She writhed, spewing blood from her lips and eye-sockets until she finally ran down.

It was like every vampire movie Kaylee had ever seen. Except the poor girl wasn't a vampire. And this was *real*.

Rob tried to withdraw the poker but couldn't.

"We need guns!" Kaylee cried out. Any moment now more dead-but-alive college kids were going to come barreling down this hallway.

"I think old Carruthers is helping Mandi!" Rob said as he continued trying to wrench the poker back and forth until its point popped out of the floorboards and then out of the now-dead girl. It was covered in gore.

"Yeah, I don't think so. You see how he looked at her?"

"What the hell do you think? I mean, he's Jason's *dad*!"

Kaylee said, "I don't know Jason. Chances are he was just back there trying to take a bite out of some big lunk like you."

Rob wiped sweat and blood off his forehead, his hand lingering as if holding his head together. He thought maybe he *had* seen Jason staggering around, blood all over him. "Damn it, we've gotta get her back."

"Gotta get out of here first," she pointed out.

"Yeah, but...how? This is all fucked up."

"Guns'll help!"

"I know where there are some, but Mandi—"

And then two more crazy-eyed dead kids turned into the hallway between them and where Carruthers and Doug had taken Mandi. Even Rob could see there was no way they could fight through the two monsters and then pick up Mandi's trail. What was that weirdo Carruthers doing? He couldn't deny it looked funny, the way he'd taken naked Mandi out of the bathroom, like she was his...*property*.

"Follow me!" Rob said and Kaylee had no choice.

Rob was trying to force himself to believe that Carruthers was saving Mandi, and that idiot deputy was helping him, but he just couldn't. There was something else going on here.

Come to think of it, Carruthers hadn't seemed all that upset at what was happening at his house. Which meant Kaylee was right, that he was somehow involved.

Rob and Kaylee went down another long hallway that led to the rear of the house. It would meet up with the other hallway and the kitchen, but you had to go through some sets of doors. Jason had just given some of his football buddies tours earlier that day, so Rob knew where he was going.

"Where the hell are we—"

"The library," Rob said, as he pulled open a set of carved doors that must have cost a fortune.

Kaylee screamed.

A monster who'd been just inside growled and reached out for Rob, grasping at his t-shirt, and Rob whacked him on the head with the now-bent poker, but it bounced off with very little effect. The guy had been NFL-bound offensive lineman Calloway, and he was three hundred fifty pounds on his light diet days. His eyes were crossed and he growled again and didn't let go of Rob, instead reeling him in like a thrashing fish. Rob's arm was throbbing from the bounce-back but he managed to draw back the poker and stick it into Calloway's right eye.

"AAAGGHHHHH!"

Rob yanked the point out, getting a faceful of bloody vitreous jelly and aqueous humor. Before the dead football player could react in the slow, methodical way most of them were reacting, Rob thrust the poker's point into the left eye-socket with the same result.

But Calloway did not stop clawing for Rob's face, and he was forced to back off and regroup.

Kaylee squealed, "Get him!"

"Trying!"

The dead player's mouth was wide open as the dead kid tried to find something to bite. Rob gave him the poker—point first, with as much of his own two hundred pounds behind it. The kid's jaws tried to bite it, breaking his teeth like ice cubes, but Rob's thrust upward sliced through the palate and presumably past the nasal cavity and into the brain.

Calloway wound down like a robot with an off-switch, and Rob shoved aside the body like a sack of empty flesh.

The library was impressive, like the rest of the house, but Rob made for one wall where an ornate cabinet had been built-in. Behind the glass door on one side was a rack of rifles, and on the other were pegs holding handguns. He used the poker to jimmy the lock, destroying the wood, and selected a medium handgun for Kaylee—it looked like a .357 Magnum revolver with a 4-inch barrel—and then he pulled a 12-gauge pump-action Remington shotgun off the rack for himself. The rifles were useless. He needed up-close and personal with lots of damage. *Thank God my dad's into trap-shooting*, he thought. He rummaged around the drawers below the gun racks, finding a couple boxes of ammunition for bothe guns.

"Put as many of these in your pockets as you can," he said as he handed the pistol rounds to Kaylee. He did the same thing with shotgun shells full of buckshot and some that were rifled slugs. *These should come in handy*, he thought. *It's like a fucking zombie movie. Good thing I've watched enough of them.* Of course, he hadn't ever expected killing teammates and friends. *Fuck'em, they weren't very nice people, most of'em.*

He was thrilled to see that Kaylee had already started loading her revolver. He did the same with shotgun.

They turned around and three monsters rushed them before they could even raise their guns.

CHAPTER NINETEEN

Mandi thought her arms were going to get ripped out of their sockets. Whoever was dragging her along wasn't very gentle. Her vision was blurry. It looked like that good-looking guy, Jason's father? He owned the house. Her memory was patchy. She knew where she was and what was going on now—except for those screams and growls from down the hall, what was with that?—but she wasn't at all sure how she'd gotten there and what had happened to her before that girl was putting her in the tub. Come to think of it, why was she just wearing a big plush towel and nothing else?

There'd been blood to wash off. That was it.

But whose blood?

She thought her head was going to bob right off her neck as the guy pulled her down a narrower hallway. The guy behind her, he was a cop. Wearing a uniform. Had his gun out. *Whaaa? Where are Anna and Krystal? Where's Danny? Where's Tyler, did he ever show up?* When she pictured Tyler she felt a jab through the top of her head, like a lightning bolt, but she didn't know what it was. Maybe it was the pills she'd gotten. *What pills? And why?*

"Come along, Mandi, my dear," the man pulling her said in a suave voice that hinted at some tension. She could relate. "We have an important appointment to keep."

"Then why am I naked?" she blurted out, half-giggling. She couldn't help it.

There was a loud crash behind them, and screams.

"Stay and wait, Doug," said the man. His hair reminded her of that actor her mom liked. Richard Gere. "You know what to do."

"Sure. Think it'll work?"

"Leave the thinking to me. He'll be drawn to her like a moth to flame. You point him in the right direction. Lead him if you have to."

Doug nodded subserviently.

Carruthers opened a door that seemed to be disguised as a utility cabinet and pulled her outside.

"We'll be there soon, Mandi." He flicked the towel she was wearing. "Better keep this on you for now. It'll be chilly where we're going."

"Huh, okay," she said, but something serious was trying to break through her mushed-up mind. A serious thought, or fear, or something she should be worried about. What about Tyler? What about the rest of her friends?

Mandi had no choice but to keep up. Jason's dad had a very long stride, and his one hand had trapped both hers and pulled her along as if she were a doll. She noticed his fingernails were very long, for a man.

Then they were outside in the evening coolness and she shivered.

Glass was breaking behind them. Smoke started to billow out of the broken window.

The grass was cold on her bare feet.

There was sudden fear in the pit of her stomach. And for the first time she realized that Tyler wasn't coming to save her.

Tears formed and ran down her cheeks.

CHAPTER TWENTY

Jesus, it's the running backs! These guys hang out together even when dead...

It was the only thought he had time to process before the monsters were upon them, snatching at their arms, their jaws opening and shutting like those of sharks.

Rob understood way down deep and on the surface too that these were no longer his friends and teammates. They were, in fact, dead and had somehow come back to life. Or some kind of horrible life, anyway.

One of them had a caved-in skull, another had been stabbed with something, and the third appeared to have been gnawed-on by several sets of teeth.

Rob's shotgun fired and took off the first guy's head.

Sorry, Antonio.

A blast from Kaylee's Magnum took care of the second attacker, perfect shot through Manfred's forehead that splattered his brains all over the hallway.

The third guy, Dwayne, was lifted off his big feet by a rifled slug from the shotgun and a Magnum round from the revolver, and tossed down the hall like a ruined rag doll.

"Mandi!" Rob said. "Have to save her."

"Okay," said Kaylee.

Then they were running.

There were more teammates coming for them, and their friends whom they'd invited to the party, and their girlfriends, and the hangers-on of all the social cliques that intersected with the football team.

151

They could smell smoke now, and an alarm started blaring somewhere behind them.

At the rear of the big house was some kind of den. Rob picked up a solid-looking straight-back chair and hurled it through a set of French doors. Except it bounced back at them and he had to leap to sidestep it.

"Goddamn it!" He lifted the shotgun's barrel and two quick shots demolished the doors and then they were leaping out through the jagged shards, feeling some cuts open up but trying hard to get themselves away from the carnage. Outside they at least stood a chance of running.

They made it to the trees and ducked behind some of the larger trunks, panting.

"Jesus, look!"

Kaylee turned and peered around the wide trunk of an old pine.

Now smoke was pouring out of several windows they could see, and they could hear screams from those few who might still be alive along with the fire alarm's screeching. But they could also hear grunts and the sound of smashing furniture overtaking the screams, so it wasn't hard to imagine the dead kids were "winning."

Two bodies hurtled through the French doors. One was a half-naked cheerleader Rob had dated one awful evening, and the one chasing her was the team's walk-on punter, whose clothes were covered in blood and gore.

As they watched in horror, the screaming girl was brought down like a calf in an arena, but instead of tying her up the punter's mouth tore into her belly and started to eat her intestines. Her screams faded and she was dead.

Now he knew why he'd never liked punters. Rob made a snorting sound as if snot were running from his nose, then stepped out from behind his tree and approached the two figures on the grassy slope, blasting them both with slugs from his shotgun.

Hope you're at rest now, he thought.

Another kid, one he didn't know, came flying out of a window, landed on his feet like a cat and lunged for him, claws extended and mouth open to reveal a horror show of blood and broken teeth.

Rob shot him in the head.

Jimmy Renalli. They'd been best friends in grade school.

For the next ten minutes, Rob and Kaylee *liberated* four more college kids from whatever had infected them and turned them into slavering monsters.

"We can't get them all," Rob said, nose twitching from the gunfire haze around them. "May not have enough bullets. And who knows how many more there are."

"You think the whole world is ending?" Kaylee thought about her parents and wondered what they'd be like as zombies. They'd fit right in. Maybe she could go home and *liberate* them too.

"I dunno, but if I can save Mandi…"

"Got a hard-on for the girl, huh?"

"Jesus, Kaylee!"

"Well, you do, don'tcha?" He nodded. "And she don't even know you exist?" He nodded again. "Sucker!"

Rob's face fell. He hung his head.

"Just fuckin' with ya. She *is* hot and all. I almost wanted to jump her myself in that bathroom!"

As tantalizing as that image was, Rob realized they had no idea how to follow Carruthers's trail. Had he kidnapped her or saved her? Rob was inclined to agree that the old lecher had grabbed her for himself. Even now he could be violating that perfect flesh…the images were disturbing.

"Hey, Rube," Kaylee said, mocking and bringing him back. "Why don't we at least work our way around the house, stay outta sight in the woods, and figure out where that perv and Deputy Doofus took Mandi. Didn't seem like there was a back door where they went, did it?"

Rob shrugged. He hadn't even noticed any of that. This kid was something else. A couple years older and he could see himself dating her, that was sure. She was growing into her beauty, though she'd already started to make her statements with the tattoos and tough mouth and all. But then he realized by then *he'd* be older too, and he would want...well, *Mandi*.

"Okay," he said.

They loaded up their guns from the remaining stash of ammunition in their pockets, and started working their way toward the front of the burning property. The log mansion was located far from anywhere, so the chances of fire engines streaking to the rescue anytime soon were low.

The house's exterior lights had flicked on a while back, so at least they could keep an eye on the windows. But the fire was starting to spread, and maybe everybody inside was dead or dying.

Or feeding.

Carefully they picked their steps through the undergrowth. They stopped suddenly when they heard a soft, almost gentle crashing through the woods nearby.

Rob held up the shotgun and swiveled the barrel in a wide arc, trying to see if any of the monsters were about to attack them. Large shadows seemed to flit from tree to tree, but then it might have been a trick produced by the flickering fire, the exterior house lights, and the shadows colliding.

He shrugged, not quite convinced they hadn't heard or seen anything, but they continued their slow traverse of the woods' edge until they reached a corner of one of the wings, and then had to jog across some open lawn to get under cover again and begin circling the remainder of the high log structure.

Sooner or later the thing's gonna go up like a box of matches, Rob thought.

What are we gonna find out front?

CHAPTER TWENTY-ONE

Professor Wallace slowly negotiated the long, narrow drive through the darkened trees. He wasn't sure what he would find. Luckily he'd spotted the sign at the turn-in or he might have driven in circles around the lake all night. When the house came into view he knew that his fears were well-founded.

He could hear screams coming from the cabin, which was not a cabin at all but a full-fledged lodge-style mansion built out of logs. Smoke was seeping out of several of the building's windows and the professor could see flickering orange firelight strobing through the glass as well. That wasn't a fireplace—looked more like a bonfire. *In the house.*

He was too late...

He needed a damn drink. Needed to crawl back into the bottle.

Stop it, just stop it!

Wallace let his car roll to a stop, opened the door and stumbled out in the direction of the house. "Danny! Danny Wallace!"

Walking like a man in a trance, he moved forward as if he were stuck inside a dream, or a vat of molasses, leaving his car door wide open and the engine idling.

Standing at the bottom step of the porch, watching the black smoke wafting through the screen door, the professor could now clearly hear the chaos previously constrained by the lodge's walls—fearful screams, breaking glass, crashing and smashing sounds of unknown origin, and finally an explosion of had to be gunfire.

He wasn't sure how long he waited there, in the shadows, trying to gather himself and stop needing the drink that called out to him. But the terrible sounds inside the house only worsened, and he winced when he heard what sounded like death being dealt to kids. He help up his hands and saw they were shaking.

Damn me, I'm weak.

But...Danny.

The professor propped up his courage, took a deep breath, and began to climb the porch steps that were more like a gallows.

A voice came from nearby. "Hey, where do you think you're going?"

Professor Wallace turned to look. Standing on the lawn not far from him was a young deputy sheriff.

"I'm looking for my nephew," the professor said after clearing his throat, feeling a twinge of hope at the sight of the deputy. Maybe the police was getting things under control. "His name is Danny, Danny Wallace. Have you seen him?"

"No. No, I haven't, professor. But I'd sure like to. We're all waiting for him. Now why don't you step down from there?"

How...?

"Do we know each other?" the professor asked, trying to place the deputy's face. Could he have been one of the professor's students? Filled with sudden increased trepidation, he backed down to the ground. Somehow it *did* look familiar.

"No we haven't met, Professor Wallace. But I know who you are." As he spoke, the deputy's hand floated closer to his holster. "You're kind of a legend in these parts. At least a legendary enemy to the members of the Order."

"I-I don't understand..."

"Oh, I think you understand just fine, professor." The

deputy pulled his sidearm and leveled it at Wallace. "I think you understand that you meddled in the plans of the Order a number of years back. In fact you tried to derail our plans. Too bad it didn't work. Too bad for you."

The professor backed slowly away from the deputy suddenly turned devil-worshipping psycho. He did understand now, if a little too late. His head had been fuzzy, but not anymore.

He held his hands out as if he thought they could stop a bullet if the deputy were to pull the trigger. The lawman followed him step for step, stalking him, trying to corner him. Wallace looked around for a clear way out, while at the same time hoping help would appear out of nowhere. Maybe he could make a dash for it if there were some kind of diversion. But now the deputy was standing between him and the car. Where else would he go?

"Yes," the deputy continued as if Wallace had said something. His voice had changed, had become a sinister drone. "The Beast will be pleased. Not only has the Lamb returned, but our long-awaited opportunity for vengeance has arrived as well." He raised his gun.

"Wait, wait," the professor tried stalling. He could feel the gravel on the driveway crunching under his shoes. "Clearly you don't have Danny yet. I can help you find him. You can use me to draw him out."

"We already have bait, professor. All we need you for is blood."

Suddenly the professor's back was pressed up against the side of someone else's parked car.

"Looks like you've got nowhere left to go, professor. I guess time's run out for you."

The professor felt a hot stinging pain in his abdomen before the sound of the shot registered in his brain. He clutched at his gut and felt the thick warm fluid oozing out of him, his mind still not quite grasping the finality of his situation as he slid down the side of the car to a seated position.

"Oh, yes, the Beast will be *very* pleased dying took you a little longer."

Tim Wallace looked up at his killer. The deputy held his gun steady with two hands. Its barrel pointed directly at the professor's head, he stared down the length of the slide directly into his adversary's eye.

"Time to die, Professor Wallace."

Instead of the crack of gunpowder ignited by hammer striking primer again, the professor heard the unmistakable sound of a round being chambered in a pump-action shotgun.

"You better drop that gun, deputy," a voice commanded from somewhere behind the murderous cop. "Just do it. *Now*. Drop the fucking gun."

The deputy's arm dropped and his hand released the gun. The professor could clearly see the hatred in his eyes. *A look that said: This isn't over, you maggot.*

"Take the gun," the disembodied voice said, and a girl about Danny's age, maybe younger with tattoos running up both her arms, walked into view around the deputy and retrieved the firearm from the ground where it had fallen. She held a large silver revolver too.

"What do you think you're doing?" the deputy asked. "I don't think shooting a law enforcement officer is a very good idea, do you? In fact, even holding him at gunpoint is pretty stupid."

"Well, officer Harris," the voice from behind the deputy said, "seeing as I just shot a number of my closest friends and teammates in the head at point blank range and then watched some of them rise get up again and try to kill me, I'm not really in the right frame of mind to consider the consequences of blowing your motherfucking brains out."

Wallace's belabored heart seemed to fall farther. *Danny...I was afraid of this. For years I worried. And now it's already started.*

The deputy stepped aside and the professor got a good view of the young man who'd saved him from execution.

"Are you all right?" the tattooed girl asked the professor, kneeling beside him.

"Yes. As good as can be expected under the circumstances, thank you," the professor said between gasps. He could hear his heartbeat drumming in his ears in time with the spurts coming from his wound. "Maybe not *as* good," he added, reconsidering.

"Now back up," the young man with the shotgun ordered the deputy.

"Come on, Kaylee," the deputy pleaded. "Are you gonna go through with this? I can get you leniency. I can tell them you were under duress…that he made you do it. You don't want to be an accomplice!"

"Shut up, Doug," the girl said coldly.

"Yeah, shut up, Doug," the young man echoed, his shotgun still trained on the deputy's head. "Are you okay, Professor Wallace?" he asked without looking away from the deputy.

Ah, he knows me!

"No, I'm afraid not. It was a good shot."

"Damn it, sir." Rob's finger tightened on the trigger. "I should blow you away, you scumbag."

Kaylee stood silent. She wasn't going to stop him.

"No, don't do it. You might need him later."

"Hm," Rob grunted. "Maybe, maybe not." To Doug he said, "Move a muscle and I'll shoot your legs right off."

"Have you seen Danny?"

"Not recently, professor."

"What's your name, son?"

"Rob."

"Rob, you must find Danny. I need to see him. It's of utmost importance. I think we can end all of this if I could just see him, speak to him."

"Well, I didn't see him in the house recently, professor. And I hope to God he's not in there now because I have no intention of going back inside. He might be in his friends' tent, but I can't leave Barney Fife here unattended..."

The professor watched as the tattooed girl stuck the big revolver in her belt, then looked over the deputy's handgun like a seasoned pro—pulling back the slide and letting it *snick* forward to make sure a bullet was chambered, and then making sure the safety was off. "Don't you worry about the deputy. I'll keep an eye on him," the girl said.

"Are you sure?"

"He knows what kind of shot I am," she said, motioning towards the deputy. "Why don't you ask him yourself."

The look on the deputy's face said more than enough.

"All right then," said Rob, lowering his weapon. He reached out and pulled the Maglite from Doug's belt. "I'll be back in a minute—with Danny, God willing."

160

CHAPTER
TWENTY-TWO

Kaylee was crouched beside the professor. She held Deputy Harris's 9mm semi-auto loosely in her hand. She had one eye trained on the deputy while the other watched the thick dark liquid leaking out over the professor's hand, soaking through his black t-shirt and blue jeans. She knew it was blood coursing out of the professor's wound, but in the dark it looked like overused motor oil, shiny and black.

The professor reached up and touched Kaylee's shoulder gently with his clean hand. She looked down and saw him smiling at her weakly.

"I have to tell you about my nephew, Danny," the professor said in a hoarse whisper.

"Un-hun," Kaylee replied, distractedly. She took watching Doug Harris seriously.

"No, really," said the professor. "This is important, you have to pay attention. My nephew Danny isn't exactly what he seems to be. Pay attention, young lady. What's your name?"

"Um...Kaylee."

"Kaylee. That's pretty."

She shrugged, keeping her eyes on the deputy. "Okay, so?"

"Kaylee, my nephew has a *gift*...in fact my whole family have this gift. Different gifts, really. Different but similar." He shook his head, as if he knew he wasn't making anything clearer. "They're gifts of the mind. Take me, for instance. I've always been blessed—or maybe it's cursed—with precognition, mostly in my dreams. Sometimes I dream glimpses of the future, which is why I'm here. It's also why I was here twenty years ago."

Now Kaylee turned to him, paying attention. The 9mm did not waver, however.

"Twenty years ago, my sister who also had gifts—many more gifts than me—was…*seduced* by the very charismatic leader of a Satanic cult. You see, Kaylee, my sister's *skills* made her very attractive to this man. And he used her to bolster his image and keep his sycophantic followers immersed in their delusional beliefs."

Wallace coughed and groaned, holding his wound more tightly. Then he gritted his teeth and went on. "At the peak of this madness the cult leader convinced my sister to allow him to sacrifice her son—my nephew—to seal a pact with the devil."

Kaylee's eyes widened.

"That was the day I abducted my nephew, Danny, from a place near here, on Killdeer Lake. Now I know I should have never let him return. But it had been so long. I assumed the cult had disbanded, without my sister around. Others had died or moved away. I wanted it all to be over. I wanted it so much that I let my guard down." The professor motioned towards Doug with his free hand. "I see now that I was wrong."

"Are you telling me these fucking zombies are from Satan?" Kaylee asked, suddenly rapt. The professor's words had started to sink in.

"Zombies!" the professor gasped. "Dear God, no!"

"What do you mean, no? I've seen'em. They're not from Satan? Why are you telling me this?" Kaylee rifled off the questions.

"No. If there are zombies they aren't from Satan, they're from Danny. And they aren't zombies."

"What?"

"You see, as Danny got older I realized that he had gifts too, powerful gifts. He had some of his mother's telekinetic abilities, but he also had something uniquely his own. A mental skill that I had never heard of before in all of my years of research. I named it *Necrokinesis*. He could— *can*—animate dead tissue with his mind, and he could do so with the ease at which you or I can ride a bike. Sometimes unbidden. I've been studying his *talents* at the University for the past two decades trying to understand the extent of his abilities. They are considerable. I was afraid he might hurt himself or others, so I've medicated him for years to suppress his abilities. I realize now that that was a mistake. I should have told him, and trained him to control what he had. I may have created the monster who can create monsters."

"So, wait a minute," Kaylee shook her head, but after what she'd seen in the last hour she could believe anything. "You're telling me that your nephew is bringing the dead back to life, and making them kill?"

"Not consciously, but yes I'm afraid that he is. He doesn't mean to. In fact he most likely doesn't even know he's doing it. His power is completely subconscious. It's happening because he's stressed."

"What about them going after living people?"

Wallace wiped his forehead. "I don't know. It's a by-product. Maybe the reanimated bodies need sustenance. Maybe their brains are scrambled into seeking some form of procreation. MAybe he's not just stressed, but angry and the anger is what's infecting them. If this is all happening, Danny's powers may be greater than I had suspected."

"It's definitely happening, professor," Kaylee said.

Doug laughed menacingly. "You believe any of that?" he said. "What a crock! These creatures are sent from our darklord Asmodeus to help bring the Lamb to slaughter. The covenant that was meddled with in the past has to be corrected."

Both of them ignored the cop's ranting. The professor grabbed Kaylee's arm with a weakening grip.

"Bring me Danny," he said. "I think I can stop this."

CHAPTER
TWENTY-THREE

Rob wandered through the small city of colorful tents and coolers, the flashlight beam leading him on. The campsite was awash with the shadows of the nearby overhanging trees, blocking out the scant light from star-filled night sky.

"Danny!" he called.

He knew one of the tents belonged to Mandi and the other girls. If he could just figure out which one, Danny would probably be there. It was just a guess, but...it felt right.

Rob heard a noise among the tents and he swung up the shotgun's barrel, bringing it to bear in the direction the sound had come from. He struggled for a moment trying to grasp both the shotgun's grip and the flashlight in one hand, but after some fumbling he managed to do it though the grip was ginger. He didn't see anything moving between the tents.

"Danny? Is that you?"

There was no answer.

At a tortoise's pace Rob inched his way in the direction from which the sound had come, preparing for an encounter with one of those *things*.

He heard the sound again. Like something moving, gently scraping against the nylon tent skins.

"Is someone there?"

Nothing.

As Rob crept slowly forward, listening, he could tell he was nearing the source of the sound, homing in on it. In a matter of steps he was standing in front of the tent from which the sound was emanating.

"Hello?" he stage-whispered. "I've got a gun."

No one answered.

Rob knelt down in front of the tent. He held the shotgun's grip and the flashlight in his left hand, and—setting the butt end of the stock on the ground—he pushed aside the tent flap.

He took the flashlight in his free hand, aiming its beam to cut through the tent's zippered bug screen entry. He strained to see inside.

Once his eyes were able to focus through the weave of the door, he saw Danny squatting inside the tent Indian-style, rocking back and forth.

"Danny!" he said, relieved. "It's me, Rob. Can I come in?"

Danny responded by nodding.

Rob set down the shotgun and unzipped the tent door. "Are you okay, Danny?" He didn't enter the little tent, but instead knelt and talked to Danny through the opening.

Danny nodded again.

"Your uncle is here. Do you wanna come talk to him?"

That made Danny look up, but he didn't show any interest in leaving the confines or security of the tent.

"Come on, man. He came all the way up here to see you."

"I d-d-don't w-w-want to see anybody."

"Is this about that thing by the fire pit?" Rob asked, playing it cool. He didn't want to tell Danny that Greg was dead. Killed by some fucking monster with an axe. "That was no big deal, Danny."

"N-n-no. It's everything. I j-j-just d-d-don't w-w-want to see anybody."

"What's the problem, Danny?" Rob was starting to panic. How long could he hang here? If he couldn't bring

Danny to the professor, could he bring the professor here?

"N-n-nobody likes me, Rob. I shhhhouldn't b-b-be here."

"That's not true. I like you. Mandi likes you. But we really need to go see your uncle, Danny. It's kind of an emergency."

"An emergency?" That got Danny's attention. "Is s-s-something wrong? S-s-something with Uncle T-t-tim?"

"I can't tell you yet," said Rob. He didn't want to be the one to tell him that his uncle had been shot, and he didn't want to scare the freaked-out kid into running. "You have to see for yourself."

Danny scurried out of the tent so quickly that he almost knocked Rob over. "L-l-let's g-g-go."

But then the professor's nephew scrambled back and forth, confused, unsure which way to go. It was a pathetic sight, watching the kid unravel like that. Rob got to his feet with the shotgun and flashlight.

"This way," Rob said, pointing. "And here, take this." He handed Danny the flashlight.

Rob saw the gratitude in Danny's eyes. He took the lead, making sure Danny was following close behind, and kept the flashlight beam trained on the ground in front of them as they quickly traversed the makeshift campgrounds. They made it back to their friends before long and, when he saw his uncle, Danny rushed to the professor's side. They could hear the roar of the building fire, but Danny didn't seem to notice.

"Danny!" Wallace's enthusiasm was as much as he could muster. Weak, he reached up as if to embrace his nephew while remaining seated.

Danny dropped the flashlight, knelt and hugged his uncle, not noticing the blood that saturated the professor's shirt or the bullet wound in his abdomen. Or not caring.

"Uncle Tim!" Danny tried to help the professor to his feet.

"No, no, Danny. I'm good right here," the professor managed, coughing. "I'm just happy to see that you're all right."

"Yeah, I'm f-f-f-fine, Uncle Tim."

"Good, good. Danny, you have to tell me, did you remember to take your medication? It's very important."

Danny gazed down at himself incredulously. The stains left on his own shirt and arms seemed very bright. "I-I-I—" he stammered. "Uncle Tim…"

"Don't worry about me, Danny. *Did you take your medication?*"

A loud crash came from the house suddenly, disrupting their conversation. They turned to watch as a thick pillar of smoke suddenly billowed out of what was left of the mansion's windows, which was immediately followed by a blast of intense flames. The ceiling seemed to have collapsed in the main wing.

"I hate to interrupt this sweet fuckin' family love-fest," Rob said, "but we've gotta get away from the house."

"Okay, okay," said the professor. "Help me up."

With difficulty, Rob and Danny helped the professor up. "Uncle Tim!" Danny yelled. "Y-y-y-ou're b-b-b-adly hurt!"

Behind them Kaylee said, "Don't get any ideas, Deputy Doug. Come on!"

The group moved together: Professor Wallace, Danny, Kaylee keeping Deputy Doug at bay with his 9mm, and Rob with the shotgun. Slowly, carefully, Danny helped the professor to a large tree across the cluttered lawn, setting him down to lean against its trunk.

"Good, good," the professor said, hunched over in pain. "Now Danny…"

"Aren't you guys forgetting something?" the deputy blurted out, interrupting.

They turned to face him. Kaylee raised the gun, squinting at him Eastwood-style.

He made a *Whoa!* Gesture and grinned luridly. "Your friend, *Mandi?*"

Rob's stomach sank. He hadn't forgotten her, exactly, but in the heat of trying to reunite Danny with the professor he had...

Yeah, he had forgotten. *Goddamn it!*

"She's with the Beast right now, in preparation for the summoning!"

Rob remembered seeing that bastard Carruthers, Jason's dad, taking Mandi. But he'd managed to convince himself the old fuck was taking her to safety!

"M-M-M-Mandi?" Danny cried out.

"Where did he take her, *Doug?*" Kaylee spit out the deputy's name with disgust and brought the gun to bear on his forehead.

The deputy laughed.

"Where's Mandi!" Rob demanded. He gripped the shotgun tightly. "You can talk with only one leg, you fucker, and maybe you can talk with only one arm, too. Or you can keep both and talk now, your fuckin' choice."

Deputy Doug smirked, even as Rob hefted the shotgun in the direction of his left leg.

"One, two, three, *fuckface!*"

But before Rob could even start to squeeze the trigger the deputy took a step back, his eyes bulging like party balloons, the smile instantly wiped from his face and replaced by an ugly grimace. He gasped, clutching at his throat, trying to dig his fingernails into it as if to remove an invisible rope. Blood welled up in bubbles along the imaginary line of the tightening rope and then started flowing rapidly in rivulets. Impossibly, his eyes bulged even more and it looked like his fingers were now scooping out chunks of neck flesh.

Danny spoke slowly, all trace of a stutter gone. "*Where. Is. Mandi?*" Emboldened by his rage, he stepped forward, coming closer to the deputy who was gargling blood now, splattering it around him as it flowed also from his nose and his ears and his eyes. His big body stumbled sideways and he was about to collapse.

"*Where. Mandi? Where. Mandi? Where. Mandi!*"

The two seemed connected by an invisible membrane, through which *something* was happening.

Kaylee's eyes were wide with fear and amazement, the gun forgotten in her grip.

Was *Danny* doing this? Rob wasn't sure, but it looked like it. *But how?*

"Danny, don't!" said the professor. "*Let him go!*"

"Let him speak, Danny," Kaylee said, finding her voice. She didn't yell but tried to sound convincing. "He's the only one who knows where to find her right now."

Did Kaylee know something he didn't? Rob thought. Was he the only one who didn't understand what was happening? *What the hell...*

Something else was going on now. Danny was staring at Doug, his hands up as if he were holding him physically. Or if his hands were ripping into the cop's neck.

But there was plenty of space between them, and Danny's hands could not be physically be doing anything to the deputy.

"Please, Danny!" The professor's weak voice managed to cut through.

Then suddenly Danny dropped his hands and Doug stumbled forward with a great gasp and a scream, collapsing to his knees and almost on his face. His neck was a mangled mess of torn flesh and running blood, but he was breathing shallowly again.

The deputy took a couple long minutes to regain his breath, wheezing like a throat cancer patient. When his voice returned it sounded like he was speaking through a voice box implant. "I can take you to her," he croaked. "I know where she is. I'll show you..." Then he erupted in a spasm of bloody coughing.

"Don't go, Danny!" said the professor, trying to make his nephew understand. "It's *you* they want. It's a trap!"

"Show us, Dougie," Kaylee said derisively, dropping the handgun to her side.

The deputy nodded with difficulty. "Follow me." His voice cracked. "Mandi…"

"Danny, please," the professor said. "They'll kill you. That's been their plan all along."

"I have to save Mandi, Uncle Tim."

Jesus, the kid's stutter is gone. Rob shook his head, not sure what he'd just witnessed. Or heard.

The pressure that had been placed on the deputy relented completely, and even though his neck was bleeding profusely now, he managed to straighten up with effort. No one helped him. "Okay," he said finally, "follow me." He beckoned the group with a weak wave of his hand. Blood dripped from his fingers.

"Danny! No!" Professor Wallace pleaded, but it was too late. Danny had already begun to follow the deputy to the Beast's lair.

Kaylee scooped up the flashlight and scooted close behind, the deputy's gun centered on his back. "I'm not afraid of shootin' you in the back, Dougie," she said gleefully. "So don't make a wrong move."

"Are you going to be okay?" Rob asked the professor.

"Don't worry about me," he responded. "The bleeding's stopped," he lied. "I don't even know your name."

"It's Rob, sir. I was in your Intro to Parapsychology class last year."

"How appropriate," Wallace managed. "Hope you liked it. Please follow them, Rob, make sure Danny is safe."

Rob nodded. "Yes, sir. And yeah, I really did enjoy the class. Guess I'm doing the graduate seminar tonight, all at once."

"Indeed, my boy. Good luck."

Rob still didn't completely understand what was happening, but he knew it was his duty to make sure Danny, Kaylee, and Mandi came home safe and sound. He wasn't sure about himself, though. He hefted the shotgun and grasped it tighter.

"Thanks," he said. "Will do." He set off after the others.

CHAPTER
TWENTY-FOUR

"Come, girl," the Beast said as he led Mandi into the subterranean ritual chamber. His voice was low and carefully modulated, guaranteed to keep her in the dark. *She has no idea what's in store for her.*

"Where are we?"

"Somewhere safe, my dear," the Beast replied.

She glanced around the antechamber with curiosity, but when they passed through the carved doors her eyes widened.

The other members of the coven—those who were able to make it on short notice, roughly a dozen in number—were already present, wearing their black cowls and holding sputtering candles. They chanted quietly, the dissonance jarring in Mandi's ears. It was as if they didn't understand melody and harmony.

The torches were burning in their evenly-spaced sconces. Both altars were ready.

"Who are all these people?" Mandi asked. She slurred her words a little, the sedative still affecting her speech though it had mostly worn off by now.

"They are...*friends*," Sebastian Carruthers, who was also the Beast, answered. "They are here to help us achieve."

"Achieve what, Mr. Carruthers?" Mandi realized she was feeling dazed, queasy, and *slow*. Slow-witted? It wasn't like her. Where was Tyler? Why was that a blank? Had he ever made it to the party?

The Beast noted that his answer must have been enough,

because when two of the black-clad cultists took her from him and led her to the altar, she went along without protest. The girl's head tipped to the side drowsily.

She really is quite lovely.

He had become aware of her beauty tonight, her bloody nakedness and vulnerability. Her lush lips and cat's eyes played up, but artfully smeared by the time she was in his house. She had even *smelled* of sex. He'd been aroused then by the whole picture, and now he was aware that his body had reawakened its desire. Painfully so, he noted, as his erection throbbed below.

The Beast quickly shucked his clothes and donned his blasphemous goat-headed robe.

It was almost time.

One of his devotees approached. "Your unholiness," he said with his head bowed, features hidden in the shadows of his hood. "Where is the sacrifice?" He recognized the voice of Sheriff John Harris.

"He will be here soon," the Beast said. "Prepare the altar."

A pair of acolytes stripped Mandi of the towel she still wore over her shoulders and anointed her with scented oils. She did not protest, her head nodding.

The Beast watched, the breath hitching in his throat. This was the best part of it all, wasn't it?

Mandi's youthful breasts were firm and perfectly shaped, the nipples neither too large nor too small, the tips hardening now in the chamber's chilly atmosphere. The Beast licked his lips and forced himself to be patient.

Then the acolytes slipped a black robe just like theirs over her arms, pulling the hood up over her head. Now she looked just like one of the others, except for the spill of dishwater blonde hair that peeked out of the hood.

The Beast joined the circle and joined the cult in their dissonant chanting, soon taking the lead so his sonorous voice soared above them all. Their evil hymn rose in volume until they reached a fevered pitch of pleasantly screeching dissonance. The Beast waved his hand and their cacophonous choir abruptly halted in mid-phrase, replaced by a deathly silence. Only the torch flames could be heard licking at the air currents as if tasting them. The flames, and unseen wraiths moving in and out of the shadows.

The coven's excited voices rose for a moment then quieted again.

"Bring the girl," the Beast commanded. "Our main altar."

They pulled her robes down, letting them drop to the chamber's cold floor, and brought Mandi to the first altar, its stretched leather surface awaiting her.

"Huh?" Mandi said drowsily. She tried to look at her surroundings but her heavy lids fended off the attempt. "*Wha...?*"

The cultists handled Mandi's sedated form and draped her face down over the altar, her arms dangling over its edges, her legs spread beckoningly wide. She began squirming in protest as much as her slowly awakening muscles and senses would allow. Four of the black-clad worshipers held each of her limbs to assure that the ritual proceeded without incident.

"What's going on?" Mandi's brain had just made a connection, perhaps hazily realizing that she was in some kind of danger. "What are you doing? *Tyler?*"

The Beast opened the front of his robes, exposing his naked erect loins.

"*Not Tyler,*" he mumbled derisively. "Not at all, my beauty. Much more consequential."

Two other cult members walked toward the Beast, flanking him on each side. One was male, the other female. They knelt and began to stimulate their leader's genitals, alternating between the use of their hands and mouths, until his member gleamed in its fully erect preparedness, ready to consecrate the altar.

It's great to be the Beast, Carruthers thought. It had always been so.

Kneeling on the leather-clad stone between the girl's outspread legs, the Beast reached down, gripped her youthful rounded buttocks and—pulling her roughly into position—thrust himself inside her.

"Stop!" Mandi shrieked, adrenaline and fear finally bringing sudden clarity. Her head faced sideways, so she couldn't see who was behind her, but she bucked and struggled. "Oh God! Get off me!" she howled as more members of the coven dropped their robes and joined in the ancient *sex magick* ritual by descending on her breasts and feet and whichever part of her wasn't occupied at the moment.

The girl's struggles were a futile waste of energy as she had no way to escape her fate. The dozen cultists held her down and joined in with their leader after he stepped aside, shooting their seed inside and out of her. Licking, biting, touching, exploring every inch of her even as she tried in vain to avoid them. The Beast watched, pleased with how the ritual was progressing.

At length the Beast returned to finish what he had started, pumping his engorged flesh in and out of the altar until his unholy seed spilled into and over her sticky back. Then the coven members released Mandi, who managed to curl in on herself, weeping.

The Beast stepped back from the defiled altar, waiting impatiently for the sacrifice to arrive.

CHAPTER
TWENTY-FIVE

Deputy Harris led them along a deerpath behind the house. To their right, they could hear Killdeer Lake lapping at the shore. On the left, a tree-covered hillside sloped upwards.

"It's right there," the deputy said. Kaylee trained the flashlight's beam on Doug Harris to see what exactly he was talking about. The deputy was pointing and a patch of brambles in the surrounding treescape. "Behind those raspberry bushes."

Carefully, she pushed aside the thorny branches and shone the light into the shadows beyond. Just as Doug had claimed, there seemed to be a narrow cave entrance formed in the porous limestone. "Who's first?"

Before anyone could protest, Danny crouched down and slipped through the opening.

"Hey!" Rob protested.

The distraction of Danny's quick departure was just the opportunity Deputy Doug Harris had been waiting for. When Rob glanced away, the deputy grabbed for the shotgun. Kaylee flinched and ducked as the shotgun discharged into the leafy canopy above them while Rob and Doug wrestled for control of the weapon. The pair fell back and rolled down the incline toward the water's edge, disappearing from Kaylee's view though she could still hear the struggle.

Shit!

Should she help Rob fend off the deputy, or try to retrieve Danny before he got lost in the cave? Not a great choice!

Then Rob called out weakly, "Get Danny and Mandi!"

176

Apparently he had the situation under control, and made her decision for her. Kaylee turned her attention to the cave.

The uneven ground near the cave entrance gave over to an old hand-carved set of stairs that spiraled downward a short distance. She could hear Danny just a few yards in front of her and slightly below as he slipped down the wet steps. Then he must have reached the bottom, and the ground was hard-packed dirt or rock. She negotiated the last few slippery steps, holding Doug's handgun in one hand and the Maglite in the other.

Kaylee trailed behind Danny, who was running pell-mell through the tunnel despite the lack of light. The beam of her flashlight was rendered inadequate by the bouncing as she ran, sometimes showing Danny, other times showing the tunnel's floor or walls—sweating limestone carved by hundreds of years of erosion.

"Mandi!" Danny called out as he ran.

She was right behind him now, trying to keep up on the slippery surface.

The tunnel was by no means direct. It turned and twisted leaving Kaylee unable to even guess which direction on a compass they were heading. At times they had to climb up small rises, and at other times the tunnel dropped off sheerly. But Danny's intensity drove them on and she struggled to keep him in view.

Before long Kaylee saw something ahead, when Danny's bounding shadow wasn't blocking it—a light glowing

"Danny!" Kaylee said in a sharp whisper. No response the first time, but the second time she said his name he slowed to a stop and turned to face her.

"W-w-what?" he asked. He tapped his toe rapidly on the cavern floor.

She wondered about the kid's thinking. He didn't know who she was, after all, other than someone who seemed to be on his uncle's side. And Rob had some sort of connection to him. Maybe he would listen. "We should go more slowly from here, Danny. We have to be careful. There are bad people all around us. You saw that Deputy Doug's a bad guy, right?"

Danny nodded reluctantly. "But w-w-what about Mandi?"

"We won't be any use to her if we get ourselves killed. You trust me, right?"

He nodded, but he still seemed uncertain.

They slowed their advance, and Kaylee took the lead. After a brief few moments staring into the distance to get a good look at the coming terrain, Kaylee extinguished the flashlight. They let the strange glow ahead of them draw them through the tunnel. About two minutes later the tunnel widened and the glow proved to be the first of a row of sconces set in the walls about ten feet apart. Each sconce held a small torch with a guttering flame.

Kaylee couldn't help but shiver in the cold and creepy tunnel.

Another fifty feet of tunnel passed under their quiet shoes until the tunnel's mouth opened wider, returned to being a cave, and deposited Kaylee and Danny in the shadows at the edge of a strange large chamber. Ahead, Kaylee could see a row of broad columns that appeared like vertical stripes created out of the surrounding shadows. Beyond that, she could make out a number of people in a wide-open area that appeared to also be lit by torchlight. Behind the people was a second row of spaced columns.

And…were the people *naked?*

Jesus. They look like…

A cult!

It was like a scream in her mind, a voice trying to make sense of things. They looked like a cult, because although most were indeed naked, those who weren't were wearing black robes and hoods. But not for long, because they were shrugging out of their clothing too and joining in the general nakedness.

They heard grunts and moans that sounded like animals, but Kaylee understood what the sounds really were. Her Mama always said, "She weren't born yesserday." Well, she'd said it exactly once, but it was still true.

She took Danny's hand and led him through the darkness, but off to the side. She was looking for Mandi among the rutting people in the center of the room. They walked around the perimeter, sticking to the shadows cast by the row of pillars. By keeping to the space between the pillars and the outer edge of the chamber, they could remain mostly invisible to the otherwise occupied weirdos in the center. Or at least she hoped so.

Secret chambers and sex-starved cultists are never a good thing, not if some of her favorite movies had anything to say about it.

This must have been some kind of secret ritual going on, she thought, like an excuse for really ugly people to have sex and pretend they're getting something from it, like powers and stuff.

She shrugged. *Whatever floats the boat, folks.*

Then she wrinkled her nose. Suddenly it smelled like... raw, wet, animal sex.

She'd been in a barn with cows and horses and pigs before, so she wasn't too surprised. But this, this was *much* more intense. It almost made her gag.

Kaylee paused and waited for the urge to pass, and Danny held up behind her. Maybe he was grossed out too, and maybe he wasn't.

She heard something...something was with them in the darkness surrounding the chamber. Something that was breathing, like some kind of animal. It was so close, she thought she could feel its breath in her face. She stretched out her hand in front of her and felt nothing. A chill raced through her. *Ghosts?*

Her imagination was running wild. It had to be, right? She took a deep breath. Not that she could blame herself with the night they'd been having. She'd killed people tonight. Or maybe *rekilled* them. She suddenly believed in a lot of things she'd hadn't believed in yesterday. She knew she would probably check under her bed and in the closet for real monsters before going to sleep for the rest of her life. And she'd never look at college kids the same way, ever again.

This made her think of Rob. Was he even now following in their footsteps?

She hoped so.

She hoped he was still alive and pining for his lost Mandi.

Partially to get out of the dark and partially to get a better view, Kaylee pulled Danny along with her and crept closer to the ritual. She could now see a man wearing a blood-red cloak. It was vivid even in the shoddy lighting. And did he have on a goat's head? Gooseflesh rose on her arms and the back of her neck. Fear caused a wave of panic that took her breath away.

Danny stepped away, disentangling his fingers from hers.

"Mandi?" he called out softly, stumbling toward the flickering light as if he were in a trance, like a moth flutters to a bug-light.

Now Kaylee saw her too, curled up in a fetal position on a small stone table beside a larger stone table. It sure looked like her, and she was naked. *Stone tables?* God, they had to be altars! Mandi's shoulders heaved as if she were sobbing, her hands covering her face in sorrow and shame.

Danny continued shuffling forward, either oblivious or entranced.

Kaylee reached out to grab his shoulder, trying to stop

him before he gave them away. She was too late. By the time she reached him they were both visible in the torchglow between the columns. Before she could go for the handgun stuffed into the waistband of her jeans, two naked cultists rushed forward and grabbed Kaylee's arms.

"Let me go," she yelled, struggling against them. But they were big.

"Mandi," Danny said, concern in his voice as he advanced, oblivious, into the ranks of the coven members. When he was close enough and her condition finally registered, Danny screamed, "Mandi!"

And the force of his anger reverberated through the open space, a wave of force causing the torches to gutter wildly, sending their smoke upward in black swirling tendrils.

The goat-headed man in the crimson robes turned toward Danny and spread his arms wide. "Son," he said. "You've come home to me. To us."

Danny turned away from the crying Mandi, his eyes falling on the tall man under the goat's head.

"Come to me, my son," the man said, raising his arms like a priest.

Like the high priest of a cult.

There was a little gray soul patch on his chin, visible beneath the goat's head mask, and Kaylee recognized him. It was the man from the house who had taken Mandi out of the bathroom and disappeared. Carruthers?

"Don't go near him, Danny!" Kaylee screamed. "It's a trick!" She fought to free her arms.

Danny's gaze swiveled back and forth from the man who claimed to be his father to Mandi's curled form. He seemed confused, and who wouldn't be? But Kaylee couldn't be sure because they were holding her behind Danny and she couldn't see his face. She didn't know if he was planning to embrace Carruthers or choke the life out of him. She was hoping the latter, but his body language was enigmatic.

From behind she couldn't tell anything about Danny's response to what he saw.

"That's right, son, come to your father," Carruthers said with gentle encouragement. "Come to where you belong. Where you *always* belonged."

And Danny did seem to be moving to him, albeit very slowly. Barely lifting his feet, he shuffled forward— hypnotized by the cult leader's unnatural charisma. Was he hypnotized?

"No Danny!" Kaylee shouted, but she couldn't even be sure Danny was registering her voice.

She couldn't see Danny's face, but she could see the long dagger Carruthers now clutched in his raised hand. She swore it hadn't been there moments before.

"Danny!" One last time before she watched the dagger slashing downward. The wicked blade disappeared behind Danny's body. He staggered back and turned a bit, and Kaylee saw that the blade had been buried in Danny's chest.

"Noooooooooooo!"

Kaylee's scream went unheard as the rest of the cultists cheered as if their team had scored the winning touchdown. Naked, ugly flesh jiggled as faces laughed with joy and religious fervor at what they had witnessed.

Danny lowered his head and stared down at himself, at the damage the blade had done. Blinking rapidly, he shook his head as if trying to deny what he saw.

Now Carruthers placed his left hand behind his son's neck before pulling the knife out of Danny's chest, and then thrusting the blade repeatedly into his stomach with wet smacking sounds.

"No!" Kaylee howled, intensifying her struggle against her captors, but to no avail. Their grips were like steel bracelets.

The other cult members started chanting as a crimson pool formed at Danny's feet. A couple voices at first, then others joined in, sounding Sunday morning church music except backwards, without harmony or melody. The sound hurt Kaylee's ears.

Danny turned sluggishly and faced her, red hands covering his abdomen as if he were trying to hold back the blood that bubbled out of the holes Carruthers had just made with the dagger. His face was a mask of confusion and suffering. The pain in his eyes was so deep that Kaylee could feel her own heart breaking as she looked into them. Unbidden tears rolled down her cheeks.

She watched helplessly as Carruthers set his dripping dagger aside and pulled Danny back, wrestling him up onto the large altar. Danny didn't even try to fight it as other hands grasped his body and moved it. He was as docile and helpless as a lamb.

"Yes, very good," Carruthers cooed. "This is your fate, my son. You were conceived for this very purpose. Our promise has been kept, Asmodeus!"

The celebrants raised their voices in mind-numbingly jangling chant as the Satanic priest produced a chalice from somewhere inside his robes and tipped Danny's compliant body forward.

Horrified yet again, Kaylee watched as he filled the cup with the blood that flowed between his son's fingers.

Danny also watched with his eyes wide but unfocused. As if he were watching from afar, seeing the abomination happen to someone else. The coven's chanting rose in volume and tempo, though it became even more dissonant.

Carruthers raised the chalice in a parody of a priest's holy rites, opening his mouth to speak…

But a sour expression crossed his features, as easily followed as a shadow. His eyes wide, he stared into the darkness at the edges of the chamber. His mouth dropped open, lips trembling. Carruthers staggered forward, and when he did, Kaylee saw Mandi standing behind him, the blood-drenched dagger in her raised hand. The priest turned to face his assailant as the goblet containing his son's life clattered to the floor.

Without hesitation Mandi drove the blade into Carruthers again and again. Gripped by rage, Mandi sank the blade into the old man's crumpling body like a woman truly possessed. Over and over the blade rose and fell, spattering Mandi's naked flesh with swaths of crimson droplets. She screamed in hate and frustration, falling to her knees as Carruthers' mutilated body collapsed to the ground, stabbing him until she had no strength left and finally leaving the blade buried in his ruined neck.

The chanting had stopped and baleful screams and weeping took its place as the cultists fell to their knees.

The high priest was dead. His body was a mass of cuts and stabs, his bowels had burst out of his pierced torso, and his head was barely still attached to his spine.

Kaylee's guards had released her and now they fell to the floor like gibbering lunatics. Suddenly free, Kaylee rushed to the altar.

First she checked on Mandi, who was still kneeling on the ground in a growing pool of the priest's blood and gore. "Are you okay? We have to get out of here. Can you stand?"

Mandi didn't respond, but she did move. Very slowly she tried to stand. Kaylee crouched down, pulled Mandi's arm over her shoulder and wrapped her free arm around Mandi's waist. Mandi stood shakily.

"Think you can walk?" Kaylee asked, worrying that the shocked weirdos could at any moment decide they just had to avenge their dead leader. Any of them looked capable of committing sadistic murder.

Silently, Mandi stepped forward with difficulty. The tranquilizers were obviously still affecting her, and she had used every ounce of her remaining strength dispatching the evil bastard Carruthers. Kaylee half-walked, half-dragged

Mandi to the altar where Danny lay bleeding.

"Danny?" Kaylee said tentatively, hoping he was still alive.

Mandi finally spoke. "Oh Danny!"

Danny turned his head to face her, tears coursing from his bloodshot eyes.

Mandi sobbed.

"Danny, we need to go." Kaylee eyed the cultists, who were still aimlessly grieving. But a couple were staring at the three of them. "Can you stand?"

Danny struggled to sit up. His hands were still knotted over his stomach in a sticky red mess. He slid his legs over the edge of the altar, grimacing with every movement.

Then Kaylee noticed the wind that suddenly blew through the chamber, seemingly from all directions at once. Intermingled with the anguished cries of the naked acolytes was an unnatural wailing that accompanied the gust.

"Hurry, Danny. We've gotta out of here!"

Danny took a hand away from his abdomen and steadied himself on the edge of the altar, which caused a crimson rivulet to pulse down his stomach and pant leg. Then he hopped down off the stone structure and immediately collapsed onto the cavern's floor.

Releasing Mandi's hand, Kaylee reached down and gripped Danny's arm. "Come on Danny," she barked like a drill sergeant. "Help me. Get up!"

The wind was gaining momentum and the strange howling noise now washed out most of the cultist's cries.

With Kaylee's help, Danny managed to stand and take a few tenuous steps before he fell again, dragging Kaylee and Mandi with him to the ground.

The torches went out.

But it wasn't entirely dark. Kaylee looked up and saw a luminous cloud materializing in the recesses of the chamber all around them. It gained substance quickly and advanced like sea fog creeping onto shore.

Oh shit!

This hadn't been a simple cultish orgy as Kaylee had thought, a way for these horndogs to get it on in secret. It was gross, but she could understand *that*.

But now something was happening that defied simple explanations. Kaylee was a realist, a skeptic, and pretty sophisticated a thinker for her age (all her teachers had said so). But right now it sure looked like whatever it was that the cult had been doing and praying for—*it had worked*.

Before she could consider her next move the glowing mist had engulfed them, swallowing the room. It ate all sights and sounds, devouring the world and leaving Kaylee, Mandi, and Danny alone, surrounded by the supernatural cloud. It had to be supernatural, didn't it?

For a few moments—moments that felt like lifetimes— the substance of the cloud became everything, as the universe they knew seemed to disappear behind its billowing form. In its shapelessness Kaylee would have sworn she saw tormented faces arising and vanishing again in the swirling ocean of unearthly light.

And it brought the cold with it, too. Bone-chilling cold that seemed to reach right through Kaylee, stiffening her muscles and turning her stomach at the same time. A cold that froze her in place, forcing her to watch the horrors as they drifted past her unblinking eyes.

Then it moved beyond them and Kaylee's heart grasped for its normal rhythm again.

She watched the cloud coalesce over the weird priest's corpse. Once it had amassed, the gaseous substance began to pour itself into the dead body through the gaping dagger wounds. The corpse started to bounce on the chamber floor, like a puppet with tangled strings.

Fear held Kaylee in place. Certainly she wanted to continue their flight, though she had no idea how she would get her disabled companions through the labyrinthine tunnel. Helping one of them would be hard enough, but helping both of them would be nearly impossible. Plus she was afraid to turn her back on the fog and whatever it was doing to Carruthers' bouncing cadaver.

Soon the last wisp of vapor had vanished into Carruthers and a thunderous sound boomed through the ritual chamber, causing the torches to flare then quickly diminish to a sickly blue flame.

What was left of the coven assembled in a ragged circle around the body. On their knees, the cult members bowed their head to the ground before their dead priest. Kaylee watched in disgust as Carruthers' body rose to its feet.

But it was no longer Carruthers.

Whatever unholy perversity had brought the flesh back to life, maybe it couldn't differentiate between the dead tissue of the priest and the old dried meat of the goat head. So it had given the appearance of life back to both of them, and somehow fused their flesh, giving birth to something with a head that was partially human and largely animal. And the crimson cowl had become a mane of long blood-red hair sprouting from the goat's head and the man's shoulders and cascading down the full length of the thing's back. Its face was an amalgam of Carruthers's and the dead goat's, with eyes that blinked red.

This wasn't a magically animated corpse—it was a demon in the flesh.

Evil incarnate.

Kaylee shivered violently.

One of the thing's worshippers rose to his feet. It was Sheriff Harris! "Lord Asmodeus, we have summoned you to offer our services to you in life and in death. We ask for nothing in return save the tools to best do your bidding… *aaaaack!*"

The sheriff choked as the demon gripped him around the

throat and lifted him off the ground.

Then the demon pulled the dagger from its own neck as if it had been reposing in its scabbard, and in one swinging arch cleaved a semi-circular gouge in the sheriff's torso from pelvis to sternum.

Harris struggled uselessly for a moment before his entrails spilled out through the incision and hit the floor with a hot *splat.*

The remaining cultists ran, scurrying off in all directions. Without their high priest they could no longer control the *thing* they had summoned, Kaylee guessed. The mostly naked cultists vanished into the shadows. The demon let them go, uncaring, but trained its human eyes—which stared out through a goat's sockets—on Kaylee and the others.

"Get up!" she screamed at Danny and Mandi. "Come on! Get up!" She tugged on Danny's arm, trying to drag him to his feet. But they were just too hurt and sedated.

In two long steps the monster was on top of them. Paralyzed with fear, Kaylee was unable to tear her eyes away from its horrifying visage. The bloody dagger clenched in its right fist, the demon grabbed at Kaylee with its left hand. She flinched, fully expecting to die.

Then the beast quickly pivoted away and blocked an axe with its arm just before the axe-head could cleave the demon's skull in two. The tip of the axe's blade took a chunk out of the creature's forearm but the axe handle delivered the brunt of the blow.

The demon stepped aside. Kaylee's mouth hung open when she saw an old blackened skeleton, its ribcage still caked with hard-packed earth, wielding that axe. Mandi screamed suddenly, "It killed Tyler!"

Kaylee made the connection, not that it mattered. Where in hell—*literally?*—had this other walking corpse come from?

The two monsters squared off and circled each other.

Kaylee knew this might be her one and only chance for survival. She heaved Mandi to her feet. Then she reached down and yanked Danny's arm. She couldn't budge him.

"Come on Danny!" Kaylee yelled. "Get up!"

"You g-g-g-go!" Danny shouted, barely able to lift his head from the cold stone floor.

"No Danny. Come on, let's go!"

"N-n-no! G-g-go on without me."

Mandi recovered her voice. "Please Danny. Come with us!"

Now silent, Danny clutched his belly in the near dark. Kaylee tried to jerk him to his feet, but he was dead weight. Finally Danny turned his head. "Go!" he snarled. "Go, you both get out of here!" Then he fell back, curling in on himself against the pain.

"Come on!" Kaylee threw Mandi's arm over her shoulder and dragged her, screaming, back to the tunnel's mouth where they had entered.

Her eyes adjusting to the dim blue torchlight, Kaylee saw more of the walking corpses assaulting the naked cult members. Many of them she recognized from back at the house, football players and their girls and buddies and cheerleaders and their boyfriends, most of them naked or half-naked and gnawed here and there, or gun-shot and splattered with blood and brains.

The new arrivals made their way to the center of the chamber to engage the demon who wore Carruther's body like a cloak. He and the axe-wielding thing were locked in a mortal embrace, trying to bring axe and dagger to bear.

Near the entrance to the cave she saw Rob, who was using the shotgun like a club, pounding a cult member's head into an unrecognizable mess.

"Rob! Rob!" she called out, excited to see her rescuer again.

But he didn't respond, instead turning and spastically

moving toward the melee near the altars to join in the epic struggle taking place there.

Rob was dead now.

Rob...

There was no time for sobbing. When Kaylee and Mandi reached the tunnel, she turned and looked back at Danny. He hadn't moved. Beyond Danny's prone body she could make out the demon, who had been that bastard Carruthers, beset on all sides by the horde of animated corpses. It had to be Danny, who had summoned all the dead he had raised today.

She wouldn't want to bet on which side was going to win the fight. She just wanted to get out and away from here before whoever was victorious turned their attention back on Mandi and her.

Kaylee had left the flashlight back in the ritual chamber, so the girls moved as fast as they could in the near dark, then having to feel their way in the utter darkness of the actual cavern tunnel after there were no more torch sconces. Her ears tuned to any sounds of pursuit, Kaylee kept her hands on Mandi, helping her up and down the dips and rises in the passageway.

Then she was helping Mandi up what she hoped was the steepest climb they would have to make, pushing her up from below, encouraging her, "You've got it. Just grab hold of something. I'm here. Pull yourself up."

They heard an explosion behind them in the tunnel and the ground shook, sending them both crashing against the rough walls. Recovering, now Kaylee worried about a cave-in. "We've gotta get out before it comes down!"

Then she felt a rush of wind accompanied by a cloud of limestone dust that peppered them and coaled the girls' skin in damp powder that stuck to their skin. Kaylee could taste it on her lips.

There must have been a partial cave-in behind them. But it was a mixed blessing—the collapsed tunnel would prevent them from being chased down by either the demon or the corpses, but this part of the tunnel could collapse, too, and trap them down here. Or even worse—crush them under tons of rock and dirt.

"Keep running!" she yelled, pulling Mandi.

A long rumble behind them seemed to indicate the cave-in was rolling toward them.

They stumbled on in the darkness.

It had to have been Danny who caused all this. The professor had claimed the kid had some kind of powers... if so, then he might still be alive. Then again, who could survive such a huge collapse?

Kaylee pulled and pushed Mandi, who was now more capable of moving on her own, and they pressed on through the passage. More rumbling behind them caused fresh concerns.

But then she sighed in relief when they finally saw moonlight filtering in through the cave's mouth.

A few more unsteady steps and they reached the opening and walked out into the night air.

More rumbles behind them, and maybe some human screams, came to them from the cave's opening. A cloud of limestone dust puffed out, and then there was silence. It was as if the ground had swallowed up the whole unholy mess of people and monsters—and people who had been monsters—and taken them all back to hell where they belonged.

Thanks, Danny...

To their left, Killdeer Lake still licked at the land, though there were visible ripples in the surface.

Killer Lake...

Now I get it.

In all other directions, tall trees reached for the moon, a bright silver disk that hung overhead like a lightbulb.

They kept to the edge of the lake basin and followed it around until they could see the lights from the house, then they cut through the woods. Occasionally large animals shifted in the dark undergrowth, and a terrible stench wrinkled their noses, but they saw nothing. If it was more of the walking corpses, they were going elsewhere.

When they reached the lawn, Kaylee saw the house burning. It was a raging inferno now with flames flickering high into the sky above the peaked rooftop. There were some piles of burning debris in scattered places on the lawn which—as they approached—Kaylee realized were bodies. Probably more of the zombie corpses, and she hoped they were really and truly dead.

Maybe Danny had killed them all at the same time.

As they reached the line of cars Kaylee tried to open their doors one by one. All were locked, except for Professor Wallace's car, which had idled itself out of gas.

"What the hell is wrong with people?" she said, mostly to herself. Mandi was teetering, almost in no condition to reply. "Doesn't anybody trust anyone anymore?"

She came to a large, low motorcycle and found that its keys were still in the ignition.

"Bingo!"

Kaylee saw the professor leaning against a tree nearby—was this where they'd left him? It seemed like months ago, but was probably less than an hour. "Stay here," she said, and Mandi nodded weakly. She jogged over to the tree.

"Professor!" She knelt beside him. "I could only find keys for the bike, but we'll send help."

Professor Wallace nodded stoically, his hand still cupped over the wound in his chest.

"Danny?" he asked.

Kaylee shook her head.

"I didn't think so. I can't *feel* him anymore. But I felt one large disruption in his *field*..."

"Are you gonna be okay? I'll send help, I promise."

"I'll be fine. I'll just sit here and enjoy the fire," he said, smiling with difficulty. He reached into his coat with his free hand and produced a small flask. He deftly unscrewed the top with his fingertips and took a healthy sip. "You girls go. I'll be fine."

"Okay. Sit tight."

He nodded and smiled. His head tilted a little, and his hand dropped the flask.

Kaylee wiped a tear that suddenly sprang up. He had done his best with Danny, but in the end the kids had created a monster. And their elders had created their own.

She shook her head. What a waste. *On the other hand...*

Kaylee returned to the bike, where Mandi swayed drowsily. Kaylee tipped Mandi's chin up and looked at her face. She was still beautiful in spite of everything she'd gone through. Kaylee leaned in and kissed Mandi's lips until Mandi opened her eyes, smiled, and cocked her head so she could return Kaylee's kiss with increasing fervor. Kaylee pulled away, smiling. Mandi smiled too and the grime seemed to melt off her face.

"We're gonna make it," Kaylee said. "Are you ready?"

Mandi nodded.

Kaylee jumped on the bike and waited for Mandi to slip on behind her. Then she turned the ignition and kick-started the engine. The Harley rumbled to life.

"Hold on," Kaylee instructed before picking her feet up onto the pegs and motoring down the gravel drive, leaving Killdeer Lake behind.

She hoped forever.

Mandi's arms around her felt more comforting than anything she could remember. There was a lot of road to travel, and now she could.

OVERTIME

It was the unmistakable rumble of a Harley engine that caught Anna's attention—but she couldn't tell if it was coming or going, or where exactly where it might be as it echoed through the woods. She pushed herself upright from the tree she'd been leaning against and lifted her head hopefully, the tears finally having dried on her cheeks from what felt like days of crying (except it couldn't have been) as she'd stumbled in circles, lost in the dark that had come up so quickly now that it was late summer.

For the thousandth time she admitted she should have just stayed with Jason.

She could have cursed him out, refused to give him what he wanted there in the woods, his shorts lowered for her supposed delight, but stayed with him instead of storming off into the unknown. Or she could have just sucked his dick and gotten it over with. It certainly wasn't the first time her temper had gotten the better of her common sense, and it probably wouldn't be the last.

She wasn't familiar with the area, and she'd barely *seen* the famous Killdeer Lake. So she'd stormed away from the horny Jason in a blind rage. But Jason was her reason for going, damn it.

And her cell phone was definitely still in the tent. Now she remembered putting it down.

Ever since her little scene she'd been wandering in the woods, getting attacked by trees, shrubs, bugs, spiderwebs, and who-knew-what (she didn't want to know). Didn't help that she was dressed for that damned rich-folks' kids' pool party, wearing tight cut-off jean shorts and a strapless hot-red string bikini top with which she'd hoped to harness Jason's attention. No wonder the bugs had been having a feast, with all that skin exposed. *Stupid.*

And then there was that weird smell, and whoever had been lurking around her in the woods. Maybe it was Jason, playing with her. Maybe other kids, trying not to get caught fucking. Maybe it was something else. She knew *one* thing.

She'd probably never go near the damn woods again.

Ever.

The growling motorcycle *was* getting louder and she started to carefully pick her way through the tangled growth, moving in the general direction of the sound. Between the shadow black spaces that had to be tree trunks Anna saw brief flashes of light—like a lightning bug's mating dance—but this was no bug, it was a motorcycle's cyclopean headlamp. She hastened her pace.

Stumbling forward in her sandals, she caught a glimpse of the bike flying by on the local asphalt road just as she reached the edge of the woods.

Damnit!

All this time she'd been only a few yards from the fucking road.

"Hey!" she yelled. "Wait!" She waved her hands above her head while running out onto the road, hoping the biker would somehow notice her. There were two people on the bike, but neither of them saw her in the mirrors. Or they didn't care.

Was the passenger naked?

Maybe...

But they were past in barely a second. The single tail-light grew smaller and smaller until the bike followed a gentle curve and the red ember blinked out.

But at least now she was standing on a ribbon of fairly smooth blacktop, confident that she would either be able to find her way back to Jason's house or help would come along soon. She sucked in a deep breath and exhaled with relief.

She hated the woods.

She really did.

Now, which way back to Jason's house?

Anna looked the pavement up and down as if hoping it

would rise up like a cartoon snake and tell her which way to go.

Crap, snake. Didn't want to think about snakes. Were there snakes in these woods?

After an indecisive moment, she struck off randomly, hoping there really was such a thing as *woman's intuition* and that it was now guiding her.

She was so relieved to be out from under the trees' spreading leaves and under a wedge of dark open sky, that she forgot how angry she'd been at Jason and his entitled rich-boy act. The fear of being lost in the pitch black, spooky woods melted away as she strode along the edge of the narrow two-lane. Soon she'd be drinking with her friends and her wilderness adventure would be a funny story to tell at future parties.

After another half hour's walking along the tree line she'd almost lost hope of reaching Jason's place, or maybe ever again seeing another human being, when a set of headlights materialized ahead of her, coming her way. She waved her hands above her head, bouncing up and down, making herself as visible as possible.

Hard to miss a half-naked girl.

The pickup truck slowed and pulled onto the crumbling asphalt shoulder, stopping across from Anna. She strutted in front of the truck's low beams to the passenger side door.

"Hey, thanks a lot for stopping," Anna said after tugging the door open, aware of the driver's gaze.

He grunted as he turned her way. He was obviously a country boy, overweight, wearing a pair of coveralls stretched over a ratty white tee and a cap covering his scruffy hair. Though she normally liked the rugged look, in this case she thought the black stubble that covered the lower half of his face gave him an almost unclean look. He was what her friends—and her—would call a *redneck*.

He was staring at her.

But who wouldn't be? Given the circumstances...

"Need a ride, do ya?"

With a nervous chuckle and fervent nod she climbed up into the truck and avoided slamming the door, rather closing it gently. The truck was old, but maybe it was a classic. Why ask for more trouble? It wasn't as if she had a more appealing offer. She didn't want to wander the dreaded countryside all night.

"Where ya headed?" the redneck asked, his voice gruff but not unkind.

"It's the Carruthers' place? Umm... Jason Carruthers? On Killdeer Lake?"

"Not familiar with it, miss."

"It's a giant house right *on* the lake."

"Lots of giant houses around the lake, miss."

Anna slumped in the seat. *What now?*

"I tell you what..." the redneck enunciated slowly, "I can take you to this bait shop we got just up ahead some, you can call this Carruthers fella, and if he can give you directions, I'll take you there. Or he can come pick you up. Don't make no difference to me."

"That would be great. Thanks."

He put the truck into gear by wrestling a huge shift lever on the column and glided out to middle of the road. "My name's Jeb, by the way. It's actually Jebediah, but everybody just calls me Jeb." He extended his right hand sideways, and Anna noticed that his hand was small and gnarled like wood. His whole arm was withered. Worse, it was dotted by thick layers of scraggly hair growing in tufts from a dozen ugly pustules. It must have been some kind of congenital abnormality. A birth defect of some kind.

"I'm... my name is Anna." She shook his hand awkwardly, reluctantly.

She hoped she hadn't been staring at his arm. It kind of freaked her out, but she didn't want to make Jeb feel self-conscious. Fortunately he either didn't notice, or she'd played it off well. Then again, he didn't seem like the self-conscious type. He put that small, knobby hand back on the wheel.

"So, Anna, you mind if I turn the radio back on?"

"No, not at all."

Jeb turned up the volume on the truck's old fashioned broadcast radio and a scratchy blend of fiddle, banjo, and pedal-steel guitar emanated from the speakers. She wasn't a big fan of country music, but it wasn't entirely foreign to her either. She'd had a couple of boyfriends who'd listened to this stuff. In fact one of them had taken her to see... *hmmm*... Florida something or other. It wasn't too bad, just didn't have enough of a dance beat.

"So, what are you doin' out here, Anna?"

"I was out at this big party and I wandered off and got lost in the woods."

"A little too much to drink?"

"No! I got into an argument with someone."

"Sounds like boyfriend troubles. Not that it's any of my business." He took the gross hand off the skinny wooden wheel to make his point.

"No," she shook her head. "Not boyfriend problems, just boy problems."

Jeb chuckled and it sounded like a clucking chicken. "I don't mean to laugh miss, it's just that you're so darn pretty that you probably have lots of boy problems."

The thought of Jeb being attracted to her made Anna's skin crawl. "No, not really," she said curtly, brushing off the comment. So much for him just being a nice guy.

He seemed to get the point. He stopped making conversation and just drove.

But the comment hung in the air, and she started worrying. Who knew where he was taking her? Where the hell was this bait store? She should have asked. How long would she have to be missing before her friends realized she was gone? How many places were there out here in the boonies to hide a body where it would never be found? She squirmed in the seat, wondering if she should push the door open and jump out, make a run for it.

Her fingers twitched as they approached the door latch almost on their own. She hoped he couldn't see from his seat.

The truck suddenly slowed as its headlights flashed on a bullet-riddled stop sign and Anna could see the same decrepit gas station they'd stopped at on their way to Jason's place. The familiar sight made her think that maybe Jeb wasn't so bad after all.

"Well…" Jeb drawled, "looks like it's closed."

She sighed loud enough for him to hear.

"Don't you worry, miss, old Ezra's place is just acrosst here. I'm sure he'll let you use his phone to call your… friends."

She looked over at the farmhouse tucked a ways down on the other side of the road, remembering how creepy it seemed when they'd stopped for gas. It looked at least twice as frightening now. Like a place you wouldn't spend the night for a million bucks.

Gravel crunched under the bald steel-belted radials as Jeb pulled the creaky truck into the terrifying house's driveway. "You look like you seen a ghost," he said. "Don't be afraid. I'll come to the door with ya. I've known Ezra my whole life. He looks scary, but he ain't half as bad as he seems."

The hillbilly wrestled his girth out from behind the wheel and stepped out of the truck, rocking it.

Reluctantly, Anna followed suit.

What have I gotten myself into now!

She walked behind Jeb as he shambled across the lawn to the decrepit front porch. The steps groaned in protest under his weight. She trailed him, staring at what appeared to be long wooden troughs lining both side walls of the house. *Pigs, maybe?* She didn't see or hear any of the animals, however, or spot any pens. Maybe they were in back. They sure looked like feeding troughs, though. And there was a smell...smelled like hogs to her, not that she knew what they smelled like. It was more a stench, a permeating foul odor that increased in intensity as she breathed it in. *Gag!* She was about to ask him about the hogs when he turned to wait for her.

She lingered on the bottom stair—worried the porch might collapse if the two of them stood on it at the same time. Jeb grinned at her crookedly and knocked on the rickety screen door with his withered hand, rattling it in its frame. "Come on up here, miss. Old Ezra don't bite."

Sighing, she joined Jeb, her eyes focused on the door even though she was worried about her feet crashing through the pint-flecked planks. She wrinkled her nose as the smell intensified.

"That's better," he said. Adding, as if he could read her mind: "Ya see, this old porch ain't gonna fall down. It's solid. They don't build'em like this any more. No, siree. It's the wood. You just cain't get wood like this any more. All the good trees been used up."

The light inside the house clicked on audibly, nearly blinding her—she'd become accustomed to the darkness under the canopy of low-hanging trees and night's falling. A grumbling voice mumbled half-awake curses as a figure appeared at the door. It was the creepy dude from the gas station. He used his hand to shield the interior light, taking a long hard look at Jeb and Anna through the screen door. At length he said, "Is that you Jeb?"

"Hey Ezra, don't mean to disturb your early evenin' slumber, but I come across this little lady walkin' down the road. She needs t' use your phone. Would that be all right with you?"

Ezra looked Anna up and down. Taking in her minimal pool-party clothes and a *lot* of skin. A crooked grin spread across his wrinkled face, displaying a few nicotine-stained teeth. "I seen you before," he said. "Get yourself lost in the woods?"

Anna slumped a little.

"Uh huh, that's what I thought. You didn't listen to me, did ya? Where'd your fancy friends get to?"

"I don't know, sir. That's why I need to use your phone. To find them."

"Well, I guess," he said, swinging open the screen door. "Come on in."

Did he just wink at Jeb?

Pervert!

Or just a lonely old man faced with an unexpected, attractive young woman?

What am I asking? There should be something in between.

Jeb held the door and Ezra stepped out of the way as Anna tentatively entered the house.

When the door closed behind her, the strange odor she'd smelled outside was cut off.

Thank God!

But then she inhaled and realized there was a sickly sweet, old-person version of the smell in here, too.

She felt a little like a fly who had wandered into the outer edge of a spider's web—maybe still enough time to get out, but the spider was on its way. She shook her head, clearing the image, but a quick look around gave her gooseflesh anyway. Even if you ignored the smell, somehow the house was even ickier on the inside.

There were stacks and stacks of yellowing newspapers and magazines rising crookedly all around the floor with narrow pathways snaking between them. Some were taller than others, but most were at least waist-high. Old black and white photos framed in repurposed barnwood hung on the walls she could see, the glass in the frames so thickly coated with dust that it nearly obscured the images. *Nearly...* She realized some nearby were portraits of freaks. Oddities. The type of anomalous grotesqueries that drew crowds at circus sideshows in a previous century. Tall, impossibly thin people. Short, stump-like people with bird-like claws. Hairy werewolf-types grinning fearsomely into the lens. Group portraits of Siamese twins joined every-which place they could be, their skin and bones fused like melted wax. The gross pictures did their damnedest to distract from the peeling, smoke-stained wallpaper and the cracked and crumbling lath and plaster walls themselves. Cobwebs spread across the shadowy corners of the room like ghosts hiding from the light.

The place was just this side of a carnival of horrors. Such a cliche, almost as if they'd planned it. But who would do that?

"Right this way," Ezra—*the spider?*—said, pulling Anna from her waking nightmare. "For the phone?" he added, as if he had to remind her.

She nodded sheepishly, following the old man through the maze that led indirectly to an arch and another cluttered room beyond.

The front room had been like a trailer of coming attractions for the remainder of the house. This next section was ill-lit by the low-wattage bare bulb in the single ceiling fixture. She allowed the old man to lead her deeper into this new haunted maze. Afraid to look up—afraid to see the images in the many frames along the walls—she trained her gaze on the floor, made of wide whitewashed pine boards beneath a stained and tattered runner often obscured by more stacks of paper and junk. She watched Ezra's shoes as he zig-zagged expertly then turned and went through a doorway on the right. He clicked on a light, which then splashed a brighter swath onto the tight hallway floor. She followed.

Apparently they were going with the carnival funhouse theme, because this room was in keeping with a set from *American Horror Story.* The most obvious feature was the bizarrely colored wallpaper. Thankfully there were no freaks on these walls.

"Well, there you go," Ezra said, motioning to an old-fashioned landline phone resting regally on a spindly old table barely large enough to hold it.

"Oh, okay," she answered as if in a trance. She eyed the old rotary phone, almost confused.

"Damn it girl, don't tell me you don't know how to use a goddamned telephone. Kids these days, I swear. Here, let me show you," Ezra grabbed the receiver and shoved it in Anna's face. "You hold this part to your head and talk into it, and you dial the number like this." Angrily he turned the dial with a finger and it made a clicking sound as it rotated back to its original position. "You think you can do that?"

"Uh huh," she said, nodding as if in a daze. *What a rude asshole!*

"It's almost time, gettin' late," the old man said. Apparently he was talking to Jeb.

"Yassir, I know, but we got a good start."

She ignored them for a few seconds and stared at the dial hoping the numbers would come to her. Hell, she didn't know any of her friends' numbers from memory, they were saved on her cell phone. Normally she just had to stab a virtual button: *Mandy, Krystal, Jason, Mom.*

While struggling to come up with the number to one single person she knew, her attention was drawn to another photograph, this one perched on the small table beside the phone. It was an informal black and white family candid. Clearly the man in the picture was a younger Ezra, with dark hair and slim build. But his teeth were still fucked up as he grinned broadly for the camera. Beside him sat a woman with long, dark, straggly hair. She was looking away from the photographer, with a sad faraway look. After noting the woman's somber expression, Anna gasped—the woman was a quadruple amputee, propped up in a chair for family picture day. In front of Ezra and the woman stood two young boys who were also physically deformed. The larger of the two had a harelip and misshapen head. The smaller—presumably younger—boy had a hairy, withered arm.

It was Jeb.

Jesus, they're not friendly country neighbors...they're father and son!

"Dumb bitch," Ezra said from behind her, barking a laugh. "You ain't even smart enough to know there ain't no *dial tone* on that phone!"

She pulled the dead phone away from her ear, studying it for a moment as if she'd never seen one before, then slowly returned it to its cradle. The damned hicks had tricked her. Her situation was deteriorating rapidly, going from bad to worse to *fucked-up-and-I'm-really-fucked* worst. She'd have given just about anything to be back in the woods right now, walking in circles until the sun came up. Nothing out in the woods scared her as much as these two suddenly did. She felt the chill drop down into her bladder.

The creepy old man was still chuckling as she pivoted to face him.

And both his sons.

Ezra's hideous teeth were prominently on display as he stood grinning like a mechanical toy monkey slapping a pair of cymbals together. Flanking him were his two sideshow offspring. Jeb with a deathly serious look on his pudgy face, his gnarled hand stuffed into the pocket of his filthy bib overalls. And the other one, the bookend to this horror bookshelf, towered over his family in a blue and red flannel shirt that looked two sizes too small. Grey hair almost concealed the unusual shape of his head at the edges of his weirdly shaped bald spot. His harelip curved otherwise somber features into a savage snarl. His arms seemed unnaturally long.

They were rejects from the goddamned *Addams Family*.

But this was no funny television show. Images of bones and skulls buried in the cellar flashed through Anna's brain like strobe-lit slides and she imagined it wouldn't take much to add hers to the collection.

After they were finished with her...

"Git'er, boys!" Ezra pointed, as if they couldn't tell who the prey in the room was.

The abominable brothers advanced on her and it might have been hilarious in a bad zombie or hillbilly serial killer movie.

But this was her life, they *looked* like zombie hillbilly serial killers, and she wasn't waiting around to see the credits.

Anna made a sudden move. She hurled the old fashioned telephone at the big one. It bounced off of his chest innocuously and fell to the floor with a loud *clang*.

She turned to run—eyes scanning for the exit—but a large hand clutched her left arm just above the elbow. She tried to wrench away, but the giant of a man's grip was like an iron cuff clasped around her bicep. Still trying to wrestle herself free, Anna went on the offensive. She swung her free elbow backward blindly with all her strength—hoping to connect with something fragile, maybe her assailant's throat. Instead her bony joint struck Jeb—who had maneuvered himself behind her—on the bridge of the nose.

She relished the cringe-inducing *Crack!* that rang out.

Jeb whimpered as he fell backward, flattening the tiny phone table and sending the creepy family portrait flying and crashing against the wall.

Serves him right!

But now the big guy grasped her right arm with his free hand. She went all-out psycho on him, but despite her fighting, kicking, and struggling, the mutant redneck held her fast at arm's length, easily avoiding her flailing legs.

Ezra chided, "You might as well quit fighting, girl. Ezekiel there has never lost anybody once he gets his hands on'em. My boy's as strong as an ox." He cackled like an old witch. "And you," he said to Jeb, "get your fat ass up off the floor. You are absolutely worthless."

"Hey, I found her, Pa!" Jeb protested. He struggled getting to his feet, using the wall to steady himself, trying to cover his crooked, bleeding nose with his shrivelled hand.

"And that's all you did," said his father with a snarl. "I told ya it's almost late!"

The big guy—*Ezekiel?*—held Anna in front of the old creep, apparently awaiting further instruction. They weren't mental giants, not by a long shot. Ezra was looking her up and down, this time ogling her openly with an ugly leer.

Seizing the unexpected opportunity, Anna swung her foot up with all her might, kicking old Ezra right in the balls.

Shocked, the old man gasped as all the air inside him was sucked out and he doubled over, clutching his tenderized package with both cupped hands.

Too late, Ezekiel yanked her back to prevent a repeat performance.

"You bitch!" Ezra finally managed to croak, his voice barely more than a hoarse, pain-filled whisper. Then he pointed out the door and down the hall. "Take her downstairs with the others."

She started to struggle, and then it sank in.

The others?

"Let me go, you fucking asshole!" She wriggled to free herself from Ezekiel's grip as the brute dragged her through the doorway and down the hall toward an open door and whatever the darkness behind it concealed. Presumably downstairs and *the others*.

Were they alive? Or dead? And would she end up joining them?

Her struggling was fruitless. What the ugly man-monster lacked in the handsome department was compensated by size and strength. She hadn't even managed to loosen his grip or force a break in his stride.

When they reached the open door at the end of the hall, Anna could see that it clearly did indeed lead to a darkened staircase down to a dimly-lit basement below. She threw her legs up and propped her feet against the doorframe like a dog trying to stay out of the vet's, halting their progress dead, but it wasn't more than seconds until Ezekiel pulled her back away from the frame, twisted her sideways, and thrust her forcefully through the opening—shoving her down the stairs ahead of him.

Her defense foiled, Anna continued struggling half-heartedly against the big man's hold on her. She knew she had little chance of escape while his enormous mitts encircled her arms with plenty of length to spare. She stumbled down the rickety steps with her feet barely touching them as Ezekiel maneuvered her like a rag doll. Once or twice her head smacked the slanted ceiling, but never hard enough to do more than cause a momentary friction burn. Then she almost tripped on her own feet when she finally reached the bottom, held up only by the brute strength of the monster who grasped her.

Jesus.

The smell.

It was the first thing she became aware of as they exited the staircase, other than the dingy lighting provided by dust-covered bulbs hanging bare just overhead.

She gagged.

Yes, there was the standard dank, mildewy scent of

an unfinished basement. But there was something else, too. Something sweet and sour, sickening, immediately unrecognizable, yet somehow familiar to a primitive part of her brain. Something frightening. Different from what she'd smelled outside, the hog-smell. This was different, sweet, vomit-inducing.

She knew what it was without question and without a doubt.

The brutish abomination named Ezekiel carried her past a group of metal boxes and cylinders with pipes jutting out of them heading across the low ceiling in all directions. What were the things her father had always talked about in the basement? Furnace, water heater, fuse box… that's what this batch of pipes must have been about. She'd never really paid attention to that stuff because in her parents' house it was all hidden behind paneled walls.

Quickly dodging through the array of strange monster-like devices, Ezekiel marched Anna into a cramped area lit by another dust-coated bare bulb hanging from the ceiling joists by a twirly cord. On the bare concrete floor was a haphazard heap of leaf-patterned camouflage clothes, the type worn by hunters in the fall, on top of which sat the largest flashlight she had ever seen. Beyond the mound of clothes and jammed up against the wall sat a chest freezer and small table stacked high with tools: hammers, clamps, screwdrivers, wrenches…and a rifle. Perpendicular to the workbench a pair of chugging refrigerators formed a partial wall that obstructed her view of the more brightly-lit space beyond.

"Hold it there, Zeke." Jeb's voice came from behind them. Clearly her benevolent driver was following them down the steps. "We gotta get her hands cuffed."

The giant stopped, still holding Anna by the arms like a doll. She was mostly standing on her own, but off-balance thanks to his relentless grip. His arms and hands seemed so very long. Jeb tumbled down the steps and landed beside them, holding a pair of handcuffs. He laid his good hand on his brother's shoulder.

"Fucker!" Anna yelled suddenly, kicking at that chubby mutant for all she was worth.

But it wasn't much, as she couldn't get enough leverage to make the kicks count.

"Whoa, ornery! Pin her down, Zeke. Let me get these cuffs on'er."

The big man pulled her close and leaned in on her. Her kicking radius further reduced, Anna folded, her body pinned under Ezekiel's great weight as Jebediah slapped the handcuffs onto her wrists right in front of her face. His crazed eyes stared into hers and she flinched away.

"Alrighty now," Jeb said, patting his brother's shoulder. He pointed at something ahead of them. "Go hang'er up."

Ezekiel kept a tight hold on his captive adding to Anna's claustrophobic sensation of being contained. Though he had shifted her around, she was no less a prisoner. In fact, her situation was markedly worse now that her hands were cuffed. She hadn't seen *that* coming.

But maybe you should have…

Yeah, ever since taking the ride on the pick-up, her life had paralleled that of every idiot sacrifice in every low-budget horror flick she'd ever seen, and she'd fallen for it anyway.

The misshapen brute pushed her ahead of him and his brother, shoving her past the old refrigerators—which were humming like transformers on a high-voltage transmission tower—and into the next room.

Before her mind could even grasp the full reality of what she was seeing, the scream escaped her throat. And it continued until all of the air had been pushed out of her lungs. Then she fell silent, gasping for air. Her skin had turned ice-cold as the blood seemed to freeze in her veins.

The throb in her ears might as well have been a drum on the moon, because it no longer seemed to be made by her own heart.

There, in the center of the room—harshly lit by fluorescent tubes set in a fixture suspended by chains set into the joists that supported the floor above—was a butcher block the size of a dining room table, and on the block was what remained of a man's body; naked, headless, limbless, the torso was pried open like a tin can and emptied of all its organs. A massive butcher's cleaver was embedded in the table top near the remains, its blade smeared with congealed blood. Behind the table a second body hung inverted from a pair of hook-ended chains set into the ceiling. This victim was also beheaded and gutted, but its legs were tangled in the hanging chains, its flaccid arms draped across the cellar floor.

But where was his head?

"*No. No. No. No!*"

The words grew louder and louder as they burst wetly from Anna's lips, unbidden. She struggled using new-found strength.

But it was no good.

Jeb chuckled behind her.

Ezekiel picked her up and placed the short length of chain that attached the handcuffs over a large nail that had been driven downward at a forty-five degree angle into the house's main beam. There she hung by her wrists, the tips of her toes mere inches from the floor.

"If you were any taller we'd have to have cut your feet off," Jeb said, offhandedly half-joking—as if she were somehow lucky.

Anna squirmed, mindlessly kicking and contorting until she was rendered breathless. Her efforts were useless.

"You fucking assholes!" she screamed, her voice raw.

Ezekiel ignored her and turned back to the grisly work

from which he'd been interrupted—cleaving slabs of pale meat from the corpse on the chopping block. Meanwhile Jeb stood by with a smirk on his face, enjoying the sight of her twisting in her bonds until she was again exhausted by her struggles. And when she stopped kicking, he moved in.

She recoiled when the redneck leaned closer and spoke softly into the side of her face. His hot, stinking breath seemed to cling to her skin like mustard gas. "You're pretty hot shit, aren't you? I could see that right off, when you were standin' on that road. Better than me." He slipped his withered hand up under her almost-bikini top and kneaded her breast. "Maybe we could find better use for you than plain hamburger."

The touch of that grotesque hand plus her view of the butchering finally brought up bile and she almost spewed. Instead she spit in his face.

"I'd rather die than fuck you, you dumb, ugly fuck," she said slowly so he'd get it. She enjoyed seeing him wince as the vomit-flavored saliva slid down his features.

"*Disgusting little bitch!* You don't get to choose. We're gonna choose for you. Maybe it'll be both, eh, snobby little twat? Every hole, and some we'll carve out just for the *occasion.*"

"Hey, hey, hey…What the hay's goin' on here?" Ezra materialized out of the shadows behind Jeb. The old man looked Anna up and down as she hung by her wrists, twirling gently after Jeb's grope. "What the hay," Ezra said again. "Why's her titty showin'?"

Jeb opened his mouth. "Un…" he said, before Ezra slapped him solidly on the left side of his face. Then the old man struck his fat son over and over. "You piece of shit. You know if there's gonna be any gettin' I'm gettin' it first. You don't do nothin' unless I tell you to. Do you understand me?"

Jeb didn't reply, instead he held up his good arm to protect his face from further blows.

"That's what I thought," Ezra said, wearing a smug expression as he turned to face Anna. He reached down and gently tucked her exposed breast back into her top. "I'm sorry about my boy, he don't have much experience with the ladies. You can see why. I hope he din't hurt you none."

She averted her eyes, unable to look the old man in the face. Fresh tears rolled down her cheeks following well-defined tracks. She imagined her mascara had left black streaks on her cheeks. "Please, let me go," she begged. It was more a prayer than any sort of plea.

"Aww... Now you know we cain't do that. Not now, after you seen everything. Hell, I let you go and next thing I know, that damn Sheriff Harris and his dumbass deputy-dawg son be out here pokin' around..."

"I won't tell anyone. I promise."

"You know I cain't trust no city-slicker chick like you. I got my boys to protect. Much easier to have you just disappear. Another victim of that damn lake. I told you that lake was dangerous. Kind of a shame though... You do sort of remind me of the boy's mother, back when she was young and smokin' hot."

Anna remembered the woman in the portrait near that old-fashioned telephone. The quadruple amputee.

"Yessiree, back when we were growin' up, Sheba was a beautiful woman in shape and spirit. She was a fighter just like you." Ezra gripped her face in his hand, turning her head to face him—sizing her up like a pig he wanted to take to market. " 'cept of course she weren't no Mexican."

Jesus, I'm Puerto Rican, not Mexican! And how does he know I'm not Italian or Greek or dark Irish, anyway?

Thunk!

Behind Ezra, the cleaver fell again. Ezekiel the butcher paid them no attention as he continued his disgusting chore.

Ezra dropped her face and stepped back in disgust. "But after the boys came, she didn't want to fulfill her *wifely duties*, if you catch my drift. Fought me off so bad I ended up taking her arms. That's when the boys first got a taste for the good meat. After that she kept tryin' to run off, so I took her legs. Not long after, she went to live with the good Lord above. Bit off her tongue and drowned in her own blood. I guessed she didn't care for the taste of herself. Oh well, she was a confused woman. Me, I always been sure of myself, ya know? And I got mouths to feed."

He looked in her eyes as if to seek some agreement there, but finding none he shrugged and frowned.

"Now, I'd let my boys breed ya—even though your offspring wouldn't be purebloods, like the boys—'ceptin' that you're a disgusting Mexican whore. Although that'd be okay with the others..."

The others?

There were more of them?

Ezra spat on the floor before adding: "Come on Jeb, you worthless turd. We gotta let Zeke finish up his chores. It's almost time."

The two disgusting creeps left the way they had come, back through the maze of discarded hunter's clothes and the various tanks and ductwork beneath the house's main floor, but not before Jeb gave her a wink and a nod giving the impression that he'd be down to visit her again before the night was over. They left Anna hanging by her wrists and the inbred giant hacking apart the dead.

Thunk!

Pause.

Thunk!

Pause.

Every time the weirdo brought the cleaver down, Anna flinched. And then the pause left her hanging, expecting the next hack, and then when it came she would flinch again. Imagining the cleaver striking her own flesh. Except...when it finally did, would she still be alive to feel every single sharp blow slicing into her skin, parting it like lard, and then hacking into her bones?

Her shoulders ached from being twisted at such an unusual angle, while also supporting all her weight. Her hands hurt excruciatingly as the steel cuffs dug into both her skin and deeply into her wrists.

"Please," she said to Ezekiel, trying to avert her eyes from the carnage of his night's work. "Please let me go. I'll make it worth your while, I promise." She threw in that part on the spur of the moment, not even sure herself *what* precisely she was offering.

The big man didn't stop cleaving the flesh into usable portions. He didn't even look at her or grunt to acknowledge her presence.

"Hey you big dumb fuck!" she shouted.

He ignored her.

Or at least that was what she initially thought. Then she realized that he hadn't heard anything. Jeb and Ezra had always touched the big brute, or pointed at things, to drive him into action.

Ezekiel was deaf!

And likely mute as well, seeing as he hadn't make a sound the entire time.

As long as she was down here alone with him she might be able to get out of this. At least it gave her a spark of hope.

She looked up past the cuffs, at the chain hung on the bent spike-sized nail. There was no chance of her bending that spike down so she could slide off the short length of chain that held the bracelets together—it already supported her weight with ease—*but*...but she might be able to swing back and forth and use her momentum to flip the chain up and over the nail's head.

Using every muscle in her lithe body, she started swinging her legs. *Thank God for all those years of junior and senior high gymnastics!*

Then: Don't thank anyone yet...

Keeping an eye on the oversized butcher-boy, she slowly gained enough velocity to try bouncing the chain off the hooked spike. She pushed up and tried to extend her arms over its large flat head.

Damn it!

Close, but not quite enough height.

She slipped back down, losing some of her speed. Undeterred, she redoubled her efforts.

What choice did she have? She didn't want to become hamburger on that old fucker's table after they were all done with her. If she thought too much about it, she'd just deflate and give up.

No fuckin' way.

Another try, another fail.

She breathed slowly, trying to gather herself as if sticking this landing would get her the gold medal. In this case, it would probably mean her life...

On the third try she struck paydirt, swinging the short length of chain up and over the bent spike as if she'd been destined to all along.

She landed on the floor, hard, like a sack of sharp bones. *Not exactly sticking it...* The impact knocked the wind right out of her. She gasped, trying to suck in a painful breath. Her joints throbbed sharply. Then she turned and realized that the behemoth, Ezekiel, was staring at her from across the room.

Oh fuck!

She was frozen to the spot where she'd landed.

Ezekiel swung the cleaver heavily, embedding its blade deep into the surface of the butcher's block. He strode around the table, long legs quickly closing the distance between them.

Spurred by blind panic, Anna rolled over and sprang to her feet, her chest aching from the fall. She made a break for the stairs.

Before she could manage a second step, her head was jerked backwards painfully. The butcher had grabbed a handful of her hair and reeled her in like a doomed fish.

Anna shrieked as Ezekiel forcefully tossed her. She tumbled past the old refrigerators, slamming into the chest freezer. The adrenaline surge sent her brain into action as her eyes settled on the workbench beside her. *The gun!* But she didn't have time to make a grab for it. Instead she lurched and went for the closest thing she could use as a weapon—a rusty screwdriver.

Reacting instinctively—a trapped animal—she turned, thrusting out the screwdriver's point at her monstrous adversary. Its blade caught the giant's snarling mouth, digging in and then scraping across Ezekiel's gums above his teeth before sliding sideways and punching a hole in his cheek from the inside of his mouth.

Shock filled the big man's eyes as he reeled back, ripping even more of his cheek as the flat head became a dull knife. He slapped a huge hand over his mouth and cheek as blood poured from both wounds. Turning away from her, he released a bestial scream of pain and surprise. He lingered there, frozen in agony and surprised indecision.

Making the most of her only chance of survival, Anna jumped up and drove the tip of the screwdriver into the back of Ezekiel's head, right at the base of his skull, leaving it embedded in his neck up to its handle.

The giant bellowed. Reaching backward with his huge hands, he tried to remove the tool, but each time he touched the handle seemed to intensify his agony. He moaned and grunted as he spasmodically contorted, suddenly bucking like a wild mustang. He slammed into one of the refrigerators, nearly knocking it over before falling to his knees. Then he dropped to the floor, twitching as a pool of blood formed beneath him. Squawking like some kind of animal.

Anna's heart jackhammered in her chest, threatening to

burst out of her ribcage. She'd never hurt anyone before, let alone killed anyone. Now she was a murderer. But it wasn't her fault, he'd forced her hand.

She heard footfalls tromping down the stairs. "What the hell is…" Jeb's muffled voice echoed from the stairwell.

Oh shit, what am I gonna do now?

She turned, awkwardly grabbing the bolt-action rifle off the workbench with her bound hands. Desperately she looked it over. She'd never fired a rifle before. She didn't even know if it was loaded. But it had to be, didn't it?

"*Oh Jesus-fucking-Christ!* Zeke!" Jeb came into view, but he didn't even glance at her. Instead his eyes had locked on his fallen kin. He stumbled over and squatted beside his brother, whimpering, batting at the body with his mutant hand. Then he pulled the screwdriver from Ezekiel's neck. It made a slick, wet, grotesque sound. She thought she'd hear that sound for the rest of her life.

Not that I have much left.

"Stay away from me," she said, her voice trembling. "I have a gun."

Jeb looked at her, his eyes narrowing with rage. "You fucking cunt!" He slowly rose, brandishing the bloody screwdriver like a switchblade. "You did this." He stalked toward her.

"Stay back," Anna warned.

The hillbilly grinned. "You don't even know how to use that, do ya?"

"Please. *Stop.*"

Jeb advanced.

She pulled the trigger, preparing for the explosion.

Nothing happened. *Nothing!* In fact, the trigger didn't even budge. She squeezed again and again.

Holy hell! She backed away from the deranged redneck, keeping one eye on him and with the other desperately trying to figure out what was wrong with the rifle.

Jeb cackled. He was closer now. He slapped the barrel of the rifle away playfully, toying with her with the surprisingly strong withered arm. "Whatchu gonna do? You gonna shoot me? You said you were gonna shoot me."

They circled the room, Anna stepping gingerly backwards, trying to fend off Jeb with the rifle's barrel while he stalked her with blood from the screwdriver staining his clenched bad hand.

Finally she noticed a tiny lever near the trigger. Fumbling, she flipped it. The old gun immediately discharged.

Startled, she dropped the rifle.

It clattered to the basement floor but Anna could barely hear it through the ringing in her ears. Her wrist ached from the recoil. Shocked, she saw the crimson stain spreading in the center of Jeb's coveralls. The cruel mirth in his eyes a few seconds before was now replaced with stunned disbelief as he stumbled two steps back.

"You shot me?" he moaned. "You bitch, you shot me!" He wiped his good hand over his chest and held it to his face, scrutinizing the blood as if he couldn't conceive of it. Suddenly he dropped to his knees, then keeled over onto his side.

Anna heard a step creak above her.

She retrieved the rifle, pain spiking through her wrist as she lifted its ungainly weight. In a panic, she dashed into the butchering room to buy enough time to get a grip, physically and intellectually, on the rifle. She regretted the decision immediately as she was greeted by the hunter's dismembered body laying on the slab and the no longer human husk hanging from the ceiling. She recoiled in terror.

She heard Ezra calling out.

"Boys? Who the hell's shootin' down there?"

Quickly she jabbed the rifle barrel up and into the fluorescent tubes hanging over the chopping block, sending a deluge of glass shards raining down onto the block and the horrifying remains. She hoped the darkness would help her disappear for a few precious seconds. Seconds that could mean the difference between life and death if she could figure out how to reload the damned gun.

"My God, my boys!" Ezra wailed, his pain and anger echoing through the cellar.

Anna crouched behind the gruesome table, ignoring the gore as best she could, and tugged on the bolt handle. She'd seen this done in movies dozens of times, why couldn't she get it open? Of course, the fact she was still in the damn handcuffs didn't help. And her wrist was stinging like hell, probably sprained.

In the other room Ezra was sobbing. She almost felt sorry for the old bastard. *Almost*, but not really. And not so much his sons, either. It had been their lives or hers, and they'd set the rules of the game. Had they just left her alone, Jeb and Ezekiel would still be alive. On the upside, who could say how many innocent people she'd saved by taking out those two cannibalistic mouth-breathers.

Now to deal with their evil progenitor.

Surprisingly the bolt handle suddenly slipped back, discharging a spent shell casing which tinkled like a bell when it bounced off the cellar floor. Her hands had unwittingly discovered how to open the bolt. *Now to close it again...* She fumbled with it, suppressing a curse.

"Is that you, you dirty little whore?" Ezra asked. He stood beside the refrigerators, the naked bulb backlighting his shape and casting a long shadow across the floor that made Anna tremble. As if the shadow wasn't human. "You gonna regret what you done, little whore." The shadow moved and vanished in the surrounding darkness.

Where the hell did he go?

She fought with the bolt handle. How had she got it to open? She should have been paying better attention.

"Oh, I am gonna make you suffer for what you done to

my boys." His disembodied voice felt as if it surrounded her. She was afraid to poke her head out to look for him, lest she give away her hiding place.

A new chill swept over her in a wave. Her intuition urged her to run, forget the gun.

As she rose from her crouch, inching forward, she felt something graze the skin below her shoulder. She jumped away, a tugging sensation retarding her flight, and her top fell away.

Ahead of her—mostly obscured by shadow—stood old Ezra, holding the red fabric by its string, a lunatic grin stretched across his face.

Anna trained the rifle on him. "Stay away from me," she warned.

"Oh no. I guarantee that won't happen." Ezra reached out and yanked the cleaver out of the butcher block. As he dragged the heavy blade across the block, shards of the shattered light bulb flew and sounded like wind chimes as they struck the concrete floor. "First I'm gonna cut your little titties right off, then I'm gonna feed'em to—"

"I'm serious, stay away!"

As if her desperation became skill, the bolt slid closed in her trembling hands.

"Show me what you got, bitch." Ezra was undaunted. His dead sons were apparently forgotten in the midst of his crazed blood lust. And plain old *lust*.

Closing her eyes, she squeezed the trigger. The blast might have been a stick of dynamite exploding in the enclosed space. It was instantaneously followed by loud metallic *ping*. Once again the recoil and her weak grip ripped the rifle out of her hands. Down the gun went, into the shadows. Anna stared. Ezra's mouth hung open, his eyes wide. He was shocked. Slowly, he looked down and even though Anna needed to run, she couldn't help but follow his gaze.

On the floor lay the broad-bladed butcher's cleaver. In the half-light she was sure she saw a divot or crater marring its flat surface.

A twisted smile grew on Ezra's features as he patted himself down, making sure he was still in one piece.

Anna blinked, getting it. *I shot the cleaver out of his hand! And lost the gun, again.*

Ezra barked a wicked laugh. Then he lunged for her.

She turned and ran. Leaping over the spreading crimson pool that still leaked out of Ezekiel's prone corpse, she sped her way through the room to the staircase. Behind her there was a *thump* followed by Ezra's angry cursing. "Goddamned son of a bitch whore!"

She figured he'd slipped in the puddle of his son's evil blood.

Head start. Head start. Keep running!

She shot up the stairs, slamming the door at the top of the stairwell and looking for any sort of latch or lock. *Nothing! Damn it, didn't they ever lock victims in the basement?*

Ezra yelled up: "I'm coming for you, whore!"

His reedy voice was followed by the rhythmic *thud* of his boots.

Shit.

She studied the hallway. The front door was straight ahead, wasn't it? Down the hall and straight ahead? Damn it, the details were fuzzy, but she couldn't stay here and wonder. She took off down the hall, looking for her exit.

Doors flanked both sides, but nothing seemed familiar. Or maybe *everything* looked familiar. So much so that it clouded her recollection of the details of the house. Had they drugged her somehow? She didn't think so. Maybe it was delayed shock and trauma. Maybe she'd had a stroke...

Behind her, the door to the cellar of horrors burst open with a crash. Anna ducked through the nearest open doorway.

As Ezra's heavy footfalls grew closer, she drew herself tightly against the shadows on the wall in this dark room. Too late to close the door. She held her breath and listened to the steps approaching while her eyes adjusted to the gloom. What now? She needed to think. Even if she made it outside she probably wouldn't make it far. He knew the surrounding area. He had a truck, a flashlight, and guns at his disposal. And he was crazy with anger and lust, not necessarily in that order.

She needed a better plan.

Ezra's pace slowed when he neared the entrance to the room where she'd holed up. Maybe he hadn't seen her slip inside. Maybe he wasn't interested anymore.

Yeah, and maybe the Easter Bunny would rescue her.

She bit her lip hard, half-hoping it would wake her from this nightmare out of a bad movie. But everything's based on real life, isn't it? Even when it's crazy? She closed her eyes, willing it all to disappear. She opened her eyes.

It wasn't working.

She almost choked on her held breath, but Ezra moved on, his footfalls receding from her doorway. Anna gave herself a few seconds to breathe regularly. She was in what looked like some kind of sitting room, with a couch, armchair, some small end tables with dusty lamps, a curio cabinet, and a staircase set against the wall heading to the second floor. Even here there were piles of papers and junk giving the room a filled look with no clear path.

What she really needed was the handcuff key and the keys for the truck. She wasn't sure about the cuffs, but she knew who had the truck keys. If she could somehow get back down to the basement she could turn the tables. *But how?* Try to sneak down to the basement while Ezra searched for her up here? Seemed too risky. She didn't know her way around the piles of hoarded stuff. She'd be better off finding an exit and taking her chances outside. She could attempt to relocate the front door—or find a back door—but it might be easier and more convenient to just slip out a window. Even that would be hard while the old pervert was lurking around. What if she bought herself more time by sneaking up the stairs to the second floor and gliding out a second floor window? She seemed to remember seeing a couple right above the decrepit porch. It would be perfect. She could climb out onto the gabled porch roof and jump down to the ground from there. To hell with the cuffs, she'd worry about them later.

Stealthily—never turning her back on the doorway into the hall—she tip-toed to the staircase and avoided the newspaper and book clutter piled up on both ends of each step, slipping as silently as she could up to the second floor. Moonlight seeped in through the window panes at the end of the upstairs hall, staining the dusty floor runner and cobweb-coated walls with squares of fuzzy white light. It was exactly what she was looking for. She crept forward quietly, one slow step at a time. Doors were set at regular intervals along the corridor, but they were all closed. Halfway between the top of the staircase and the window, the floorboards groaned as Anna shifted her weight. *Just what she'd been afraid of!*

She froze. And waited.

In the silence of the dark hall, the protesting floor had seemed as loud as a cannon.

Only a few more steps and she'd be clear of this hell-house. Slowly she lifted her offending foot. The groaning board called attention to her again, as if the house itself were trying to thwart her. And now she heard footsteps on the stairs behind her.

Desperately she tried the nearest door. The knob spun worthlessly in her hand, the latch refusing to catch. In blind panic, she sprinted to the next door, twisted the handle, her fear causing her to lean in. The door swung open suddenly and she fell into the room. She sprang to her feet and closed the door behind her.

In the dark, she felt along the door jamb hoping to find a lock or latch. Having no such luck she backed away from the door and turned to find another window brightening the room with moonbeams. In the glow a table sat, its top littered with more unrecognizable clutter. Anna approached, hoping to find something to use as a weapon among that crap.

Even from a distance she could clearly make out the plethora of unlit candles of various sizes and varieties standing at the table's edges, their wax now dry, frozen in strange dripping shapes like landscapes on some tiny alien world. But she couldn't make out what the candles surrounded. There was something stringy. Hair maybe? And a wrinkled lump of some sort. A pile of blankets, or sheets?

She was close now.

Her breath caught in her throat as her mind put the puzzle pieces together. What she saw in front of her, even after the horrors of the cellar, turned her sweat cold and clammy. It was a body—at least part of one—dry and mummified.

A head? Yes, but there was more...

Skin pulled taught, covered in tight creases and wrinkles. Lips stretched back exposing stained, cracked teeth. Eyes gone—empty sockets with crisp-looking lids sewn open with black thread. A thin, wattled neck like wrinkled bedsheets. And then...The deflated breasts indicated to Anna that it was the body—or just the torso—of a woman. Her second clue was the body's bare genitalia. The dried labial lips were pried open in a frozen gape as if they had been...*used?*

Oh my God! She almost snorted: *no God here! Not today!*

It must have been Ezra's wife—the boys' mother. Maybe it was a sick-ass shrine or even more sick-ass sex toy. *Or... both?*

Crash.

The door behind her flew open. Startled, Anna stumbled forward—bumping the table and overturning it. The mummified torso and half-burned candles spilled to the floor, disappearing in the room's shadows. She glimpsed a mantle of dark hair covering the torso's parchment-like skin before her attention shifted to the new threat behind her.

Like a gorilla's, her mind tossed out at her. But she had no time to process the thought.

"Jesus Christ!" Ezra shrieked. "What have you done, whore?" His hands went to cover the top of his head as if he were trying to keep it from exploding.

Enraged, he rushed her like a bull, all arms and legs.

The terror and disgust clutching at her heart gave her what seemed to be superhuman agility.

She reacted, twisting to sidestep the full force of Ezra's charge. Dodging his crazy onslaught, she ducked out of the way at the last moment.

Maybe the old man's fury at her destruction of his bizarre trophy had made him careless. Missing Anna, the power of his rush crashed him headlong into the window. Glass shattered and termite-eaten wood splintered.

Seizing her chance, Anna used Ezra's momentum to her advantage and gave him a hard shove in the back at the right moment. The old man's body continued on, flying out the jagged opening and taking out most of the wood around it. With a short scream he plummeted to the ground.

She watched him fall. The gable roof didn't extend all the way across the front of the house, and the old man caught the edge of it with his shoulder. He hit the ground with a dull *thud.*

She leaned out, careful to avoid the jagged glass knives, and stared at his still form for a full minute. No motion. He might have a broken back or neck, or maybe some serious internal damage. Even if he was alive, that second story fall *had* to slow him down a little. She had to find the truck and handcuff keys!

Anna rushed out of the room and raced down the hall. She bounded down the stairs, nearly tripping on the junk and tumbling to the bottom before sprinting to the cellar door and down into the cold damp basement once again. The whole time she was screaming in her mind, forcing herself to go back down there in the butcher shop that had almost claimed her. She shivered but swallowed her fear.

Panting by the time she made her way into the room with the freezer and work bench, she saw the brothers. Ezekiel, face down in a pool of his own blood on the far side of the room—she could see where Ezra had slipped on the blood, smearing it all around the floor. To her right Jeb lay sprawled out on his back, some blood beneath him too but much of it had soaked through his shirt and overalls, staining his entire torso crimson.

Anna sucked in a deep, calming breath through her nose. The stench of blood and spoiled meat and worse soured the air. Her hands still trembling, she stepped over Jeb's corpse. *You need the keys,* she told herself. *He can't hurt you.*

She crouched, pulled open the right front pocket of his denim overalls with a cuffed hand and reached inside with the other hand. She found a full keyring and pulled it out, trying to avoid the blood and not snag his pocket.

Then his gnarled hand grasped her wrist.

She'd been crouched over him, flipping through the keys, when he came back to life.

She dropped the keys as she leaped up, trying to wrench her arm away.

Jeb was still alive, but just barely. He raised his head and looked through her with his lachrymose, piteous eyes. His lower lip quivered as he struggled to say something, but lacked the energy.

He wasn't going anywhere.

"Let me go, you fucking sicko!"

She pried his twisted fingers off her wrist, grabbed up the keys again, looking for freedom from her shackles. Jeb's head dropped back to the floor with a sickening wet *smack*. His body twitched convulsively as the last of his lifeforce evaporated.

With a *yelp!* of joy and released tension she found the key and freed herself, tossing the cuffs onto Jeb's still chest. Then she strode into the butcher-shop, trying hard to ignore the carnage. It wasn't easy. Searching in the dark she finally found her red top, but it was slick and greasy—maybe from the film of fat and flesh that saturated every surface of the room. "I am not wearing *this*!" she said, dropping it as if it were cursed.

Shit. She shrugged. She knew clothing was the least of her problems but she willed herself to remain sane by focusing on the familiar, not the evidence of gruesome death all around her.

She spotted the rifle again. Should she should take it? Was she going to call the police? *Yes!* She probably should. But what if they didn't believe her? She'd just killed three people! And her fingerprints were likely all over this place. She'd seen plenty of unbelieving small-town cops railroading innocent people on TV and in movies. On the other hand, how could they not believe her? There were two butchered hunters here—no way she could have done that. And wouldn't DNA determine that she hadn't? If she took the gun, wouldn't they shoot her by mistake?

She shook her head. *Can't deal with all this now.* She just had to get out of this house of horrors. She'd figure it out after a shower and maybe twelve or fifteen hours' sleep.

Yeah, right. Like she could ever sleep again.

With Jeb's keys in hand she left the butcher-shop behind and headed up the stairs. Making her way down the first floor hallway by stepping around the piles of papers and strange junk, she recognized the room where she'd tried to use the old fashioned phone. It was much easier to put it all together now that she wasn't worried about being murdered and chopped into little pieces. Before long she had worked her way through the mazes and stood staring at the front door. It was at the end of the hall after all, but the junk piles had hidden it.

Or maybe it had moved around on her, like in the movies.

The door was unlocked. She swung it open and took a deep breath of the fresh night air.

But...her nose wrinkled. There was that stench again, worse even than what permeated the basement butcher shop.

Maybe these backwoods assholes did raise hogs or something? Anna remembered those troughs she'd seen when she first got here, a lifetime ago. The insulting haze was a mix of spoiled meat, spoiled vegetables, body odor, flatulence, and something else. Musky, like a wild animal. But the spoiled meat part, that was easy to understand, thinking back to that active crime scene in the basement. She'd seen a *Criminal Minds* where body parts were fed to hogs. The meat stank, the hogs stank...presto, one fine stench.

Before stepping out into the foul-smelling dark she looked over the keys, singling out the one with the old Ford logo. A cooling breeze made her shiver as it teased her bare skin, but it also made her gag because it was so...*disgusting*.

However she knew how close she'd come to never again feeling a breeze, so she couldn't help but smile tentatively. No matter how bad the hogs or cows or whatever it was stank, she was free.

Leaving the front door hanging open, she jogged down the rickety steps and headed for Jeb's truck.

For a moment she thought about checking on Ezra. He could be seriously hurt, dying in a heap of broken bones at the side of the porch. She grinned. *That's what the gross perverted murderer deserves!* But what if he wasn't there?

Then what? She hastened her pace.

She covered the short distance without incident. She tried the driver's door. *Unlocked.* Of course, who would lock their doors in the middle of nowhere?

Anna hopped into the cab and fumbled around, finally slipping the key into the very old school ignition. She settled into the sprung seat and went to turn the key...

And then a gnarled hand burst into the cab through the side window and clutched at her shoulder with claw-like fingers. The nails were lined with red, blood or raw meat. It was that same old Ezra. He'd somehow crawled up and was standing on the truck bed behind her, reaching through the window. She tried beating his arm back with one hand and finding the key again with the other, but his single arm was stronger than it had any right to be.

She screamed in frustration and rage as he grabbed a handful of her hair, dragging her inexorably through the opening.

Flailing at his arm, she grasped the steering wheel with her knees and finally found the key, turning it with her other hand.

The truck's engine rumbled to life.

As the old man pulled her head back painfully, Anna fumbled around with the column-mounted gear shift and finally slipped it into gear, any gear. It happened to be *Reverse.* She slammed her foot down on the accelerator.

With a wet *smash,* Ezra's face crashed horrifically into the window behind her. But his hand was somehow still tangled in Anna's hair.

Turning the wheel all the way to the right and jamming the stick into *Drive,* Anna made a doughnut in the front yard, the spinning tires kicking grass and dirt up as Ezra tumbled sideways into the bed's sidewall.

"Goddamn you!" Ezra hollered through broken lips and teeth, as he lost his grip on her locks. Then he slid on the

bed liner all the way back to the tailgate where he hung on for his life.

Anna had had more than enough of this bullshit. Gritting her teeth, she punched down on the brake, sending him rolling up to the front of the bed again, where he struck the back of the cab with a resoundingly wet *thud*. Then she immediately floored the accelerator again and Ezra tumbled to the back of the truck with a shriek. She cranked the wheel hard to the left, making a second series of circles in the yard, the centrifugal force pinning the old man in the corner of the bed.

Then Ezra, struggling to stand, managed to fall off the rear of the truck.

She stopped. Looking over her shoulder, Anna saw him staggering towards the front porch, gesticulating with one good arm and dragging the crooked other one.

Not this time, old man! You're never going to hurt me or anyone else ever again!

Spitting out chunks of sod, the truck fishtailed in the soil she'd freshly turned over, as she mashed the gas pedal clear down to the floorboards. She wheeled around and framed the limping creep in the pickup's headlights as she bore down on him. He turned his head at the last minute, and she may have heard him scream out "*Noooooo...!*" before the truck's grille impacted with him and he was swept under the bumper.

She could clearly hear and feel Ezra rolling under the truck's frame as she ran him over. She spun the truck on a hundred and eighty degree arc and—finding his crumpled form on the lawn—proceeded to drive over him a second time, the suspension bouncing as she crushed his body under the truck's wheels.

She drove over Ezra another half-dozen times, until he was barely recognizably human. His head was a smashed pumpkin after Halloween, his body an array of unevenly stuffed trash bags tossed to the side of the highway. He was just a big greasy, bloody, broken mess.

Not unlike what he and his disgusting offspring had done to innocent people.

Now she'd be able to sleep at night, knowing that the boogie man was dead and gone—down for the count and then some.

Anna sighed, relief overwhelming her. She cried.

It was over.

Easing the old truck down the driveway, she stopped at the turn-in. Maybe she could use the gas station they'd stopped at what seemed like such a long time ago, while on their way in, to get her bearings. Then she could probably find Jason's house and call the police.

No, *home* was what she needed. Home and a bath and a margarita or two. And a shirt. And another couple margaritas. Mandi and Krystal could tell her about how great the big party was when they got back into town. If she tried to find a phone to call the police she'd be right back where she started.

The driver's side door disappeared with a loud scream of tearing, crumpling metal.

Anna barely had time to register what had happened when a nasty odor enveloped her at the same time that a hairy fist snapped her head sideways, then grasped her left arm and whipped her out of the truck's cab as if she were a child's rag doll.

Her head burst with pain where she'd been struck and her arm popped out of its socket and there was nothing she could do, the scream frozen in her throat as the rest of her body sent her brain its pain readings.

Some kind of creature grunted over where her battered body lay on the gravelly driveway. She tried to assess the situation. After all, Anna had made mincemeat of those asshole cannibals in the house, but this, *this* was something else.

And it was worse.

Her body and her brain agreed. Besides the pain, this was *way* worse.

Thoughts a-jumble, Anna gave the last of her strength to an effort to roll to her feet, but then the shadow of whatever had yanked her from the truck enveloped her and for the first time she saw what it was.

A gorilla-like, hairy, oversize human-shaped form with malevolent porcine eyes set deep below protruding brows. Wide-open jaws full of discolored fangs. Long, hair-covered arms, one of them withered. Grotesquely large uncovered genitalia that signaled just exactly what the monstrous form felt right then.

Anna moaned, fear finally overtaking her every other emotion, erasing the pain of her dislocated arm, and filling her with a tangible dread.

This was it now, the end.

All because I wouldn't give Jason head.

She laughed bitterly, despite her grim situation.

The monster—was he some kind of *bigfoot*, whatever they were called?—tilted its head at her laugh, which was already turning into sobs. A long, gristly tongue poked out and licked mottled lips, letting drool leak onto the hairy chin. He poked her belly with a long, smelly finger. Then he poked some more.

Anna screamed.

The thing stood then, and howled a strange kind of sound that was half-grunt, too.

And more of them melted out of the trees. One, two, three of them. Mouths open, fangs clacking like castanets, drool leaking out in ropes. The stench was overwhelming, but Anna was beyond caring. One of the three was smaller, with flaccid breasts spilling onto a belly covered in fine hair. Reminiscent of the horror up in that room, where Ezra had gone berserk. *The mother? Grandmother?*

Then Anna remembered the long troughs that lined the sides of the house.

No, not hogs. The hillbillies fed their somewhat distant relatives body parts from their victims. Apparently every night, after sundown. And tonight the troughs were empty.

Empty because of her.

Anna had upset their routine, had prevented dinner from being served.

The mother made a squeaking, wailing sound and pointed at Anna.

"Yes, I'm a victim too," she told the monstrous matriarch through dry lips. She tried to make her expression sympathetic despite her terror. "I can get you food."

The mother tilted her head and stared at Anna with large, oily orbs.

Anna felt a thin tendril of hope around her stuttering heart.

But then...

The mother released a sudden stream of invective at her children. Two of them took Anna's hands in their own twisted fists and pulled.

Hard.

Anna screamed in pain when they yanked on her dislocated arm.

But they didn't stop pulling.

As Anna screamed incoherently, they continued pulling until her shoulders popped and flesh tore and they slipped backward, each holding one of her ruined, bleeding arms.

Anna fainted. Just like that, the lights went out and she was elsewhere.

Which was probably for the best, a little tiny bit of her brain whispered comfortingly as her consciousness slipped away.

Because it was dinner time. And the children were hungry.

POSTGAME

Professor Wallace reclined against the tree trunk and watched the house burn.

His gunshot wound wasn't hurting anymore. In fact his whole body felt numb and warm as he drifted in and out of consciousness. Was he even still alive? He felt a cool night breeze ruffling his hair, so maybe he was.

In the soup of his clouded mind he remembered two girls leaving on a motorcycle and the burning house collapsing in on itself.

He wondered if help would arrive. It would probably take some time. Weren't the local authorities somehow caught up in this? The sheriff? Hadn't the sheriff and his son been part of this? Maybe the whole local population. He'd thought the cult was no more, only to realize it was very much still in existence.

He held up his hand and saw the fresh black blood.

Ah, I guess there is still pain after all...

He slipped away again for a while.

His eyes fluttered open and he knew it was the end.

He was hallucinating. Between him and the burning remains of the house, he watched as a blackened skeleton carried Danny's body out of the woods and laid it onto the lawn.

That can't be real, Professor Wallace thought.

It was his last thought.

The skeleton turned and walked stiff-legged back into the woods.

deadite press

"WZMB" Andre Duza - It's the end of the world, but we're not going off the air! Martin Stone was a popular shock jock radio host before the zombie apocalypse. Then for six months the dead destroyed society. Humanity is now slowly rebuilding and Martin Stone is back to doing what he does best-taking to the airwaves. Host of the only radio show in this new world, he helps organize other survivors. But zombies aren't the only threat. There are others that thought humanity needed to end.

"Tribesmen" Adam Cesare - Thirty years ago, cynical sleazeball director Tito Bronze took a tiny cast and crew to a desolate island. His goal: to exploit the local tribes, spray some guts around, cash in on the gore-spattered 80s Italian cannibal craze. But the pissed-off spirits of the island had other ideas. And before long, guts were squirting behind the scenes, as well. While the camera kept rolling...

"Reincarnage" Ryan Harding and Jason Taverner - In the 80's a supernatural killer known as Agent Orange terrorized the United States. No matter how many times he was killed, he kept coming back to spread death and mayhem. With no other choice, the government walled off the small town, woods, and lake that Agent Orange used as his hunting ground. This seemed to contain the killer and his killing sprees ended. Or so the populace thought…

"Suffer the Flesh" Monica J. O'Rourke - Zoey always wished she was thinner. One day she meets a strange woman who informs her of an ultimate weight-loss program, and Zoey is quickly abducted off the streets of Manhattan and forced into this program. Zoey's enrolling whether she wants to or not. Held hostage with many other women, Zoey is forced into degrading acts of perversion for the amusement of her captors. ...

"Answers of Silence" Geoff Cooper - Deadite Press is proud to present the extremely sought after horror stories of Geoff Cooper. Collecting fifteen tales of the weird, the horrific, and the strange. Fans of Brian Keene, Jack Ketchum, and Bryan Smith won't want to miss this collection from one of the unsung masters of modern horror. You won't forget your visit to Geoff Cooper's dark and deranged world.

"Boot Boys of the Wolf Reich" David Agranoff - PIt is the summer of 1989 and they spend their days hanging out and having fun, and their nights fighting the local neo-Nazi gangs. Driven back and badly beaten, the local Nazi contingent finds the strangest of allies - The last survivor of a cult of Nazi werewolf assassins. An army of neo-Nazi werewolves are just what he needs. But first, they have some payback for all those meddling Anti-racist SHARPs...

"White Trash Gothic" Edward Lee - Luntville is not just some bumfuck town in the sticks. It is a place where the locals make extra cash by filming necro porn, a place where vigilantes practice a horrifying form of justice they call deaddickin', a place haunted by the ghosts of serial killers, occult demons, and a monster called the Bighead. And as the writer attempts to make sense of the town and his connection to it, he will be challenged in ways that test the very limit of his sanity.

"Whargoul" Dave Brockie - It is a beast born in bullets and shrapnel, feeding off of pain, misery, and hard drugs. Cursed to wander the Earth without the hope of death, it is reborn again and again to spread the gospel of hate, abuse, and genocide. But what if it's not the only monster out there? What if there's something worse? From Dave Brockie, the twisted genius behind GWAR, comes a novel about the darkest days of the twentieth century.

AVAILABLE FROM AMAZON.COM